Raymond Thursday's
SUITCASE

To Boyl
Best Wishes
Mike Grattan

Written & Illustrated By
Michael A. Grattan
Published By Michael A. Grattan

Typeset by Michael A. Grattan
Printed and bound by Granthams (UK)
www.granthams.co.uk
Photograph by Sarah Kennion

ISBN 0-9546736-0-3

To
Mam and Dad

Contents

1. When In Rome

Shhhhplatt! I had landed quite firmly on my bottom in several inches of snow, cold quickly seeping through and numbing my bottom. Standing I brushed the fine white crystals from my rear and rubbed my eyes in total disbelief, genuinely thinking that when I stopped rubbing them and looked around I would find myself back safely in my bedroom with Lenny.

This was most certainly stranger than my worm dream, it was bitterly cold and I hoped to wake up very soon. I stopped rubbing, and little by little opened my left eye which was met by a vision of white fields and trees topped with a fine coating of caster sugar snow.

The small brown leather suitcase was at my feet its colourful travel labels a stark contrast to the blinding whiteness. The handle was cold in my hand as I picked it up, then turned to try and get my bearings. Whuumpff! I was thrown with such tremendous force back down into the snow I thought I'd been hit by a runaway tractor.

Before I could even attempt to sit up cold steel was pressing into my chest, my eyes followed the point from the sharp tip along a lengthy blade, to a jewelled handle, up a bare hairy arm and across to finally rest on a face that would make milk curdle.

If my history books were correct this guy was dressed as a Roman Centurion!

"Excuse me mister, I seem to be lost could you tell me where..." Before I could finish his large and ugly face was inches from mine bellowing "Silence you 'orrible little Briton or I'll send you to meet your maker," his hot fetid breath smelt like old sweaty socks that had been farted into. "My Dad will thump you for that."

Whuumpff! I was prostrate on the snow again. "Bring him with us," roared the Centurion with the farty breath, it was only then that I realised he had a whole troop of soldiers with him all wearing red skirts and armour.

One of them lifted me to my feet by my hair and thrust the suitcase into my chest, causing all the air in my body to be expelled in one painful gasp. "March Briton" and he pushed me in the back to get me started, this wasn't funny anymore I seriously needed to wake up - yet I knew this was far too real to be a dream.

So here I was being marched across a snowy field by the ugliest, meanest Centurion you could imagine and his band of battle hardened troops.

Moments earlier I'd been watching a video 'The Beast from Mars' in my bedroom, with my best pal Lenny Grimes.

How did I get here, I don't know? All I can tell you is the events which led to my apparent capture by Roman Legionaires.

2. Staring Dad

I can never remember being really unhappy. My first day at school was pretty horrible, but after a while you sort of get used to it and on the whole it's okay, sometimes it could even be described as fun. Although it's hard to admit now at eleven years of age, it was probably fear that first day, to leave the safety of home and Mum, and to be thrust into a world of strange and scary children, filled me with a dread I had not experienced before.

Funnily enough most of the children were not really scary, some a little strange but most of these were now my friends and their strangeness only makes them more interesting.

One in particular was Lenny my best mate, I'll tell you more of him later.

I never told my Mum I was scared on my first day at school, if anything she was more anxious than me, Dad said she was a born worrier. Mum was very pretty and extremely fussy, before I came along she used to work in an office, typing things, I think. Her proper name was Pauline but Dad always called her Polly.

She was now officially a house-wife, this term always bothered me and had no logical sense whatsoever. I imagined Mum walking down the aisle in our local church with this huge house on her right arm, water spraying from several of the windows where the pipes had been ripped from the earth, the congregation all wearing wellies. "I do" she said nervously and the vicar pronounces them "house-wife and house."

If anything I concluded she should be called a husband-wife or a Dad-wife, this would make a lot more sense.

I know it is not really fair to all the other Dad's in the world, but my Dad was the best anyone could ever have. I am absolutely one hundred per cent certain that all my friends wanted one just like him.

When their Dad's came home from work they did boring things like going to the pub to play dominoes or worse still they studied the "Gee Gee's". Apparently this was when you wanted to gamble on which horse would win a race.

You would read about how the horses have done in their last few races, what the jockey was like and even what the grass on the race track would be like on the day of the race.

The fact that it was hard or muddy could make all the difference. This process would occupy a Dad for a whole Saturday and most of the Dad's in the neighbourhood were more than happy to do this. Thankfully my Dad had no interest at all in how firm the grass was at blah blah racecourse, and I swore I never would either.

Nearly every Saturday Dad and I would have a day out together, sometimes I was allowed to take a friend but mostly it was just him and me and that was fine. He taught me everything a boy needs to know, how to spit, how to whistle through your fingers, how to skim stones on a pond, how to ride my bike with no hands and even how to burp at will. "Don't burp in front of your Mum or we'll both be in trouble!" he said, I never let him down.

Oooops, there I go rambling on and I haven't even introduced myself, my name is Raymond Thursday but my friends call me Ray, only my teachers call me Raymond and Mum if I've been particularly naughty or cheeky.

I'm a normal kid living a normal life, in a normal town with normal parents and a nearly normal little sister and that's about all I can say about myself.

My Dad's much more interesting, he's 40 years old, but when we're together he can easily be the same age as me. Along with nearly everyone else in our town he works in the shipyard, building ships and submarines. Dad stands at exactly six foot tall, has hands the size of dinner plates and still plays football in our local Sunday League, Mum, Jo and me go to cheer him on every week.

It's not a very good football team and most Sundays they get beat, Dad says he does it for the exercise and to keep old 'father time' at bay. Mum says he's just never grown up and that is the brilliant thing about him, he's just like one of my mates...........but bigger.

His name is Roy Thursday, he wanted to call me Roy when I was born, Mum put her foot down at this idea and said it would be too confusing, one Roy in the house was enough for anyone.

So they agreed to change the 'o' to an 'a' and I became Ray. Dad said it was the very least he could do considering the amount of work Mum had to do, to get me born.

It was Saturday, Dad was busy making sandwiches for our day out, "Where are we off to today Dad, can we go to the sand hills and catch some taddy's?"

"Its a bit late in the year for tadpoles Ray, but we can still go to the sand hills if you want." "Great" I said and rushed past him to get our bikes from the shed. I loved going to the sand hills, it was in fact an old sand quarry where great valleys had been gouged from the hillsides and to me was our town's version of The Grand Canyon.

There were several ponds at the sand hills full of frogs, toads and newts. We were not allowed to go and play there on our own, as it was supposed to be dangerous, sometimes there were great sand slides not unlike avalanches on Swiss mountains. Neither myself nor my friends had ever seen one and decided it was a story parents make up, to make sure you do as you are told.

Dad put his flask of tea in his back-pack "Ready lad?" and we were off, it only took about twenty minutes and soon the red brick streets were replaced by fields and trees. We scooted down an old track with tall hedges on either side and crossed the dis-used rail tracks.

The rest of the journey had to be made on foot, after pushing my bike up a steep grassy hill the ground in front of us suddenly disappeared, green lush grass turned into golden sand. We left our bikes up against a single wired fence and hopped over the other side.

"You can go first this time Dad,"

"Sure," "Yeah, it was me last time remember?" "Great" said Dad and he ran towards the point where the field disappeared, as his foot made final contact with planet earth he yelled "Geronimo..o..o..o..o..o." I peered over the edge to see Dad sat at the bottom of a steep hill covered in sand wearing a big satisfied smile.

"Come on in the sands lovely," he quipped. I backed up and made my run as I leaped off the end I tried to keep running like they do in the cartoons on the telly, it never worked and I plummeted down until I hit sand and rolled to almost the exact spot where Dad was,

"That was great, let's do it again." Dad agreed and we leaped the same leap several times, then we found other hills to jump off, and finally we played 'Best Man Falls.' For this game Dad sat at the bottom of the hill and I stood at the top, he would then pretend to shoot me with an imaginary gun and I would fall as if shot, complete with agonising moans and cries. When I was completely dead at the bottom, Dad would climb up and I would shoot him, then we'd give each other marks out of ten for the most agonising death fall.

Eventually we both tired of clambering up hills of sand and decided to go and sit by the big pond to eat our lunch. It was like an oasis in the middle of a desert, plants and shrubs surrounded most sides of the pond and at the far end a great clump of bull rushes swayed in the warm September breeze.

Huge black and blue dragonfly's hovered, then shot off to who knows where, an occasional frog would break the surface for a gulp of air then disappear expertly to the bottom like a secret agent scuba diver and water boatmen would paddle this way and that as if looking for passengers. I loved this place, Dad loved this place, he and his friends came and played here when they were my age........

"In the olden days" I thought to myself. Then of course it was a working quarry alive with men and machinery, the men would chase you off if they saw you. But worst of all was Doc Harry, he lived in the shed with his two whippet's, Killer and Death.

If he saw you he'd let the dogs loose, then it was a race for your life to get to the top of the hill, over the fence and cycle off as quick as you could. Dad said that he and his friends would all be playing when suddenly one would shout "Doc Harry!" The hairs on the back of your neck would stand on end, you never dared look back and any second you expected the jaws of a ravenous whippet to clamp down on your ankle and hear the evil cackle of Doc Harry.

It was a game to us and thankfully a game old Doc never won.
I wished I could have been in Dad's gang, I wished Doc Harry would suddenly appear, we would escape by the skin of our teeth, Dad would be proud of me but we wouldn't tell Mum.

I chomped down the final mouthful of my cheese sandwich, took a swig of banana milk shake and looked across at Dad. This was usually the time when he would tell one of his stories. There were no stories this day, he stared out over the pond in complete silence, perhaps he was desperately trying to remember a story for me, perhaps he'd run out.

I didn't want to interrupt his thought so just watched him, the setting sun's light reflecting off the ponds surface making patterns across his face.........he never blinked. I tried it but the light made me squint and my eyes began to sting.

At last he turned to me and opened his mouth as if to speak, then stopped and returned his gaze to the pond. Without looking at me said "Come on son, lets be making tracks, otherwise your mother will have a search party out for us."

He seemed to take a huge breath, get up and trudged off up the hill to where we'd left our bikes. I followed looking over my shoulder all the time for Doc Harry, Death and Killer.

When we got home Mum asked us if we'd forgotten where we lived "Just her idea of a little joke Ray," Dad said winking and putting the bikes back in the shed.

Mum was hanging out washing "No end to it!" she muttered, while Jo threw plastic coloured pegs over her shoulder, shouting "one, one, one."

She still had an awful lot to learn, and as things turned out so did I. In the weeks that followed Dad stared that stare more and more and I found out why.

3. Stolen Tonsils

It's an extremely busy life being eleven, when I was not getting a 'proper education' as Mum called it, I was out playing with my friends.

Mostly Leonard Grimes, who sat next to me in nearly every class in school and invariably got me into trouble. Lenny had a thick shock of spiky red hair and enough freckles to fill a can of semolina pudding. He was slightly smaller than me, six months younger but very tough, nobody messed with him........he was missing one thing, a sense of fear, it was just missing from his personality.

Most evenings we'd play football in the local park often with up to twenty five players on each side, a typical match would continue until the light ran out or our Mum's would call us in.

It was horrible if you were the first to be called and for some unknown reason it was always the Mum's that did it, never the Dad's. Then the lads would start on you "Time for your bath Raymond, Mummy's going to wash under your arms and give you some nice clean undies," "Yeah and if you're really good she'll tuck you up in bed and tell you a bedtime story."

"Then your Granny will come round and give you a big sloppy kiss."

It was impossible to respond in the appropriate manner because your

Mum would overhear and she'd wash your mouth out with soap and water, or something equally disgusting. All you could do was wait for the next game, hope it wasn't your turn to be called in first, then enjoy sweet revenge, this was often more fun than football itself.

"Or, Mum just five more minutes," "No, Now," "But Mum," "NOW!" "B....." "No RayMOND, you've got school tomorrow."

The emphasis now being very much on the last four letters of my name, I knew at this point I could not win and trudged unwillingly home. You could never win, all the Mum's were the same, Lenny just laughed at everyone, he never got called in early because his Dad was out playing dominoes and his Mum wanted some peace and quiet.

If not playing footy, we'd wander off down the docks, this was a brilliant place where we'd swim all summer You could dive from the old wooden jetties and construct rafts, which we would then paddle using drift wood to the other side of the dock, we were all strong swimmers and there were no currents so it was relatively safe.

Dad came sometimes and would dive off the top jetty, I would never do this "I'll lose my shorts," I told the lads, I'm sure they never believed me, but we never pushed anyone to do something they really didn't want to.

Every now and again an old Destroyer or Frigate would come in to be scrapped, in the evenings there was no one about so we'd slip on board and have imaginary war games. On the old railway track were dis-used trains, coal trucks and guards wagons. The guards wagons were the best, this was the small carriage that would be at the end of a goods train, inside were wooden benches, a small cast iron fireplace and oil lanterns.

We'd raid our respective Mum's bread bins, collect coal from the railway lines to light the fire and make toast in our dimly lit den. Once this was done it was time to tell the scariest story you could possibly think of, the object of this was to try to make each other jump in fear, course if you did you were a wimp.

Little Dougie was always the first to lose his nerve, he'd get so fidgety and nervous it would transmit like a virus to the others, all it took now was one little noise or creak and we'd be out of the guards van like a swarm of mice who'd just seen their first cat, running in the half light across the tracks until our screams turned to laughter and grubby tears ran down our cheeks.

I suppose it was a large industrial waste land, but to us it was the biggest adventure playground in the world and I never wanted to live anywhere else.

I hadn't really noticed anything different at home, but never the less it felt different. That night as I lay in bed an air of uneasiness came over me. I tried desperately to put my finger on what was wrong............nothing ....surely there was nothing, convinced I happily drifted into sleep.

"Raymond, don't you dare interrupt me!" A massive fist slammed onto the table causing all the breakfast pots and myself to jump six inches into the air. Mum dropped a cup on the kitchen floor which shattered and scattered in a thousand directions, Jo started to screech.

I'd made an error something was definitely wrong. I sat in silence unable to move or speak, I thought frantically...........what had I done to make Dad so cross? He was talking to Mum and I was talking to him, two conversations at the same time, nothing unusual about that in our house. Unusually on this occasion he kept ignoring me, he was talking to Mum about something, I wasn't paying attention, it was boring grown up stuff, bills, mortgages, clothes for the kids.

Mum was staring now that same stare that Dad had that day by the pond, I wondered if I had it too. I wanted to say sorry, "Dad" "Go to your room Raymond," Mum said quietly.

I sat in my room listening to the muffled voices coming through the floorboards. I thought about creeping down the stairs to sit at the bottom and listen to what they were saying, I should have paid attention, Mr. Lyon at school was always saying I should. After a while I began to feel less angry with Dad and felt guilty for what I had done, although I was still not sure exactly what that was.

I opened my bedroom door slightly and heard Dad say "we'll just have to tighten our belts a bit." I shut it quickly as I heard someone climbing the stairs. Dad knocked and entered my room "Sorry Dad" I blurted feebly, "Don't be daft Ray, it's me, truth is I've been letting things get to me a bit lately with all the trouble at the shipyard."

"Anyway never mind me, how's school?" "It's just school Dad, yer know."

"And how's young Grimesy?" he always called Lenny - Grimesy, "Keeping out of trouble?" "Yeah, most of the time."

"What trouble?" I finally got to ask, Dad took a deep breath and decided I was man enough to know. "Orders are down, there's just not enough people wanting ships built anymore, to keep the yard running the bosses are making up to two thirds of the entire work force redundant, and unfortunately I'm one of them."

I looked puzzled "Redundant is when you don't have a job anymore

Ray, in four weeks time I'll be a man of leisure." He tried to be cheerful at the prospect but it didn't work.

I patted him on the back and told him not to worry, tomorrow I would go out and get a paper round, "We'll be alright Dad." I was trying my best to help, to say the right thing but I don't think it worked.

He put his big arm around me gave me a squeeze and said "Course we'll be alright." In the weeks that followed we all tried to act normally and forget the troubles at the shipyard. Lenny's Dad was to lose his job too, Lenny said "He's not really bothered, the house is paid for, Mum's got a job and it'll give him more time to study the gee gees."

He was going to buy a new car with his redundancy money and Lenny was to get a new mountain bike. I was envious, a new bike.........I wasn't really grown up but I did understand that our circumstances were different from Lenny's.

We had a mortgage, Mum couldn't work because of little Jo, so there'd be no bike for me........I was disappointed but I understood. Dad said that next Friday ten thousand men would lose their jobs in one day, there just wouldn't be enough jobs in a town our size for all those men, some would probably never work again and many others would have to leave town to find work.

Dad wrote hundreds letters applying for jobs most of them in places and towns I'd never heard of. I hoped he wouldn't get them, I didn't want to leave, and found myself even feeling attached to my school and Mr. Lyon.

Mum didn't want to leave either, she hoped it wouldn't come to that. We all stared a lot. Since our weekend at the sand hills Dad hadn't really taken me anywhere, he just wrote letters and dug the garden over and over, I think it made him feel better.

Mum said "He needs a bit of time on his own," so I never bothered him, I really did understand. I wanted time on my own when I learned I had to have my tonsils out.

It was only last year, at first I asked every conceivable tonsil question in the world, then went away and thought about it on my own. Mum bought me new pyjama's and slippers and Dad bought me the Dandy Annual. I was reading a story about Desperate Dan when they came and wheeled me off on the trolley.

I thought how brave Dan would have been in my place, in fact he would have probably done it himself, but I wasn't Desperate Dan and I was terrified. A doctor leant over me and asked me if I could count from one to ten, I was insulted "Course I can" I said indignantly, "Okay, if you can I'll buy you a huge bar of chocolate," "Easy-Peesy, one..two..three...four.....five......sixxx........sev........"

And that was the last I remember about that, after a while I woke up with a throat like I'd swallowed the sand hills, I was given a drink and some cereal and the rest as they say is history.

Things are generally never as bad as they first appear. I wanted to share this revelation with Dad, but he was too busy writing or digging. Of course the really, really good thing about getting your tonsils out is you get to eat tons and tons of ice cream, three times a day for a whole week, brilliant! The really really bad thing was the doctor lied to me, he told me he would give me my tonsils back in a little jar, that would have been so neat.

I could have taken them to school to show all my friends. I imagined them to look like large pink tadpoles and thought I might even give them both names. But I never saw the doctor again, I thought he might show up as I was leaving and present them to me for my bravery under anaesthetic.

"I bet he tells all the kids that," Lenny said when he came to visit me at home, "I bet they put them in tins of cat food or tins of corned beef, doctor's will have a nice little business going, selling other people's tonsils, probably worth at least five pounds a pair."

Lenny always said weird and stupid things, I could never figure out if he said it for a laugh or he really believed it, still he was funny.

Some weeks later I opened my packed lunch at school and found to my horror two juicy red corned beef sandwiches smiling up at me from the aluminium foil they were wrapped in. I just couldn't do it, so I swapped them for two peanut butter's off Brian Sheppard or Shep's as we called him. "Oooooooooh you don't want to be eating them," Lenny said his face contorted into a picture of puke and puss.

"My Dad says that all peanut butter is made in America and that the Americans don't really like us because of the war," "but they were on our side," "Don't interrupt," he was getting more excited now, on the verge of another one of his strange tales.

"Anyway they don't like us, and the people in the factory for a laugh flick bogeys into the crunchy peanut butter, there are approximately twenty seven bogeys in each jar."

"Can you believe it" said Dougie in amazement,
I couldn't and wouldn't, but still asked Mum to get smooth in future.

Dad's last Friday at work arrived, that evening there was to be a "Redundancy Party" in the local pub The Queens Arms, Lenny's Mum and Dad were going as were a lot more of our friends parents. During the day nearly all the Mum's made goodies for the party at night, Mum said that if I was good she would bring me some home. "I thought we were coming too," "No silly it's only for adults, lots of beer and daft grown-ups, we'll get you a nice video to watch on telly tonight."

This meant that our next but one neighbour Mrs. Kilburn would be baby-sitting us. In actual fact as a human being Mrs. Kilburn was lovely and Jo and I loved her like an adopted Aunt or Grandma, it was just, I can barely say it, she had a full set of whiskers!

Not only that but even at my age she would insist on coming up to my room and giving me a very furry kiss good night.

She must have taken a hairy pill when she was very young or eaten lots of crusty bread, I felt sad for Mr. Kilburn he would have to kiss her every night, ugh! Mum did get me a video to watch although I couldn't really concentrate, I could only think of the dreaded kiss.

Mrs Kilburns hair was pure white like candy floss at the fair ground and I saw it illuminated from behind as she crept into my room.

I shut my eyes tight and tried to create an invisible force field all around me, it didn't work the single curly white hair on the tip of her nose made first contact then splosh. "I could eat you and your little sister up for me supper" she cackled. "Night, Night chuck," and off she went waving her candy floss head from left to right and singing "If you were the only boy in the world and I was the only girl." Her voice faded as she descended the stairs and for a moment she almost sounded in tune.

When I was very young before Jo was born, I actually thought she might eat me for her supper. I'd lie there waiting, extremely cross with Mum and Dad that they'd left me in the care of a child eating bearded lady.

4. My First Worm Hole

The next morning I woke early checked my face for white curly hairs, washed my face and brushed my teeth, Mum had me well trained. She was having a cup of coffee and catching up on all the gossip in the Sunday papers when I came down.

"Where's Dad?" I enquired, at the same time peering out of the kitchen window to see if he was doing more digging.

"He's still in bed Raymond,"
she said her eyes not leaving the black and white text, "Is he sick?" I asked, I'd never been up earlier than Dad before, except for Christmas mornings,

"No, bit of a late night and one too many lemonade's that's all."
Dad would have said that this was one of Mum's little jokes. "Here, take him this cup of tea and the morning paper, he's got something to tell you."

Mum had the beginnings of a smile in the left hand corner of her mouth, like she did that time when she pretended she'd forgotten my Birthday, so I guessed it wouldn't be more gloomy news.

It struck me about half way up the stairs that this was an opportunity not to be missed. I now concentrated on my feet as I placed them on the stairs, don't make a sound, I used my will power to stop the stairs creaking, it worked on all but one stair. I placed the paper and tea outside the bedroom door and very, very slowly began to turn the handle, flinching each time it made a tiny squeak. This morning I would get him!

The door swung open without a sound and I rushed in, silently at first, but as I got nearer I launched myself into the air letting out our gang call "Ooooooooaagh!"

I was just about to land on top of him and give him the fright of his life when two huge hands emerged from the bed covers grabbed me around my waist, turned me over in mid air and threw me backwards onto the bed.

He held me down and tickled me until I could bare no more, "Stop, stop, enough you win." It just wasn't fair I thought, just wait until he's a little old man, I'll throw him down and tickle his boney ribs until his false teeth fly across the room with laughter.

"Still can't get me" he said laughing and slurping his tea at the same time, he commented on what a rare treat it was to to be waited on by a very small servant and how he could get used to this lifestyle, he was just trying to wind me up for a laugh, but I wasn't biting.

"Wait 'til you're old, I'll get you back," I saw his false teeth flying through the air again and giggled to myself.

"Mum said you had something to tell me," "I do, a bit of good news in fact, do you remember my old boss at work Mr. Pratt?"

He didn't wait for a reply,
"He has this fantastic static caravan down on the south coast just outside Abbey Forest, well he told me last night how sorry he was to lose me and that we can use the caravan anytime, for free."
"So your Mum and I had a chat last night and we're going down for a week, setting off Monday morning, what do you think of that?" I was beyond thinking, I was already jumping up and down on the bed like a kangaroo with a flea. "Brilliant!" I shouted, Dad was getting covered in tea but didn't seem to mind one bit.

I bounced all the way into Jo's room and told her we were going on holiday, as I waited for a response I scanned her face for white curly hairs, but there were none. "One" she said "No, not a single one" I laughed and raced downstairs.

At breakfast Dad explained that Lenny's Dad was lending us his old Moggie for the week before he sells it, I wondered why we needed a cat and why Lenny's dad was letting us use his, until Mum explained that 'Moggie' is a nickname for a Morris Minor, a make of car apparently.

Later that day she rang Mr. Lyon to get special permission for me to have a week off school during term time,

"Yes I see, of course I understand and appreciate your point of view, yes and sorry to disturb you at home, thank you .....bye."

Mum put the phone down gazed at the ceiling and said, as if to herself "I wonder if Mrs. Kilburn would look after him for a week," my heart sank all the way to Australia, but there it was that tiny smile appearing in that same left corner, she'd got me again.

It turned out Mr. Lyon said it was fine under the circumstances and that I might be given a little extra homework when I get back,

"I can live with that" I exclaimed and began to leap up and down again.

The Sunday before our holiday we played footy in the park as usual, fifteen on our side and sixteen on theirs, but it was still fair as they had Neil who was only half decent in nets and supported Chelsea.

I asked Lenny to thank his Dad for letting us use the Moggie. "Don't think I'll bother Ray" a worried look spreading across his face "My old feller said it had never been out of town before and it would probably pack up altogether after twenty miles." I decided not to believe him and the game commenced. We were winning 13 - 5 when Mum's voice sounded across the field "RayMOND"

For once I didn't mind being the first to be called in, the lads tried taking the mickey but their hearts weren't in it, they knew that tomorrow during double maths and geography Raymond Thursday's desk would be empty.

I've always had a real problem getting to sleep on Christmas Eve's, it was just too exciting and that's how I felt as I lay in bed. I thought about what everything would be like, the caravan, the site, Abbey Forest, the beaches, the village and even my new bedroom. I counted sheep, I counted the tall stories Lenny had told me, I even counted the bogeys in two hundred jars of crunchy peanut butter and estimated that in my lifetime I had eaten three thousand seven hundred and fifty two.

I was very poor at adding up so it could have been a great deal more. I stared at the orange patterns on my ceiling caused by the street light outside, each time a car went by its headlights caused them to shift and elongate from left to right, or right to left depending on the direction of the car.

But now there were no more cars, they were all in their garages fast asleep, why wasn't I!

I tried to think of absolutely nothing and managed it for about two seconds, the patterns on my ceiling were becoming less clear, a single bird sang in the distance. We had to be up at six!

The early bird catches the worm Dad would say, if I were a worm I'd stay in bed until dinner, the birds would have to eat bread.

I crawled out of my hole looking to the sky for birds and fishermen digging for bait, the tall strands of grass were swaying gently in the wind like waves caressing a shore. I weaved my way through the dense undergrowth when a dozen or so ants ran past me and one or two actually over me in a state of sheer panic all chattering at the same time, tiny high pitched voices "Someone's coming, someone's coming, run, run."

Then the earth shuddered a most terrible shudder, the soil around me rose out of the vegetation and into the bright sunlight I was travelling upwards on gigantic spade. Suddenly the sun was blotted out of existence by an enormous hand reaching down for me, it grabbed but I was too slippy......but no, it had me again!

Then a voice as loud as jet engine "Nice big juicy one here Bert, should catch me a cod with this 'un I shouldn't wonder," the hand began to shake me, small pieces of earth fell from my body, I tried to scream "Stop" but no sound came. It shook, it wouldn't stop shaking..............stop...........“Wake up” ....please stop.......... “Come on wakey, wakey”............stop it.......... “Raymond wake up son” It wasn't a fisherman it was Mum, it was a dream, just a dream................!

"I had a really weird dream Mum," "Not now Ray, we have to get packed for our trip." Of course it's Monday, we're going on holiday, I must have slept all of ten minutes, the excitement made me forget my tiredness and my brief experience of being a worm.

Dad teased me about being so sleepy as I crunched into a bowl of cereal "Couldn't sleep," I dribbled, "Thought Santa was coming did you, never changes does he Mum?"

I'd slept through most of the Christmas Days in my life due to being awake the entire night before, it was a standing joke in our house.

The rain gently patted the windscreen as we turned the corner of Smeaton Street and waved goodbye to Barrow-in-Furness at least for a week. I sat up front with Dad and after a few short minutes the rain patted more persistently, large circular raindrops sat happily for a second, then swish were washed away by the wipers.

"Are we nearly there yet?" "Over three hundred mile to go yet son," "Well how far had we come?" "About seventy miles, I reckon." That was

great, Lenny had told me a porky again, I could relax now, pat, pat, pat, pat, swish, pat, pat, pat, pat, swish and within moments I was sound asleep.

Dad gave me a nudge as we drove through a small village made up of tiny cottages and white washed shops, this was it Abbey Forest Village, a sign loomed out "CAMP SITE THIS WAY."

The old Moggie had made it, if only I knew then, that this sleepy little village was about to change my life in a way even Lenny couldn't have imagined.

5. The Black Hole of Mrs. Trickett

I'd slept all the way to Abbey Village which was brilliant, a four hundred mile trip passed in the blink of an eye. Dad was in reception asking for directions to our holiday home, a large static caravan set against the edge of a wooded area, an old man came out wearing a cowboy hat and pointed this way then that.

"Cheers," I heard Dad say as he clunked the car door shut behind him, "Was that a real Cowboy Dad?" "No son they've got line dancing on at the club house tonight, old Yukon Bill said we should go it's a really good night."

"Is he really called Yukon Bill Dad?"

"No, he's not son and don't you dare call him that," "Okay" I smiled, Dad was always joking around. We found our caravan straight away and as we got out of the Moggie the rain stopped and the sun peaked through a gap in the clouds, for once the weathermen had got it right Dad said squinting at the sun and turning the front door key at the same time.

The door was opening, I rushed past Dad nearly knocking him off the steps "Wow" I squealed "It's monstrous," by this I meant it was extremely large not horrible like a monster from the black lagoon.

I wanted to be the first to see everything, living room with telly

"Great," dining room "Fantastic," miniature bathroom "Neat," Mum and Dads bedroom, "Cor," my bedroom "Excellent," Mum and Dad were still standing at the door following me at high speed with smiling eyes.

Jo would be sleeping in the travel cot in the living room so I had a bedroom all to myself, it had bunk beds like I have at home for when friends stay. Best of all it had window which looked straight out onto the woods, a squirrel saw me watching him and dashed up a tree and out of sight I wondered if there were any bears in there.

When I emerged from my room Mum and Dad had already unpacked and were having a cup of tea, Mum was reading the welcome leaflet from the manager of the site.

"There are over a hundred holiday homes, a field for tents, a camp shop, a club house with entertainment every evening, a launderette, an outdoor solar heated swimming pool and shower facilities, it's got the lot," and with that she threw the tea towel on Dad's head "As a special treat Dad and Ray get to do the pots all week, I'm on holiday."

Dad looked at me raised his left eyebrow and shrugged his shoulders. Mum decided that later in the afternoon she would do a weekly shop, then the rest of the week would be free for fun and days out.

Dad said he'd take us down to the beach so Mum could get on. Mum set off with a great jerk in the Moggie, it lunged forward like the other type of moggie hunting a mouse, we laughed, she stuck her head out. "Not amusing, I haven't driven for three years." She turned her head back gave us a Royal wave and drove off quite smoothly. "That's the last we'll see of the old Moggie," Dad joked wiping a pretend tear from his right eye, we'll probably see her tonight on the telly on that Police, Stop programme.

Dad put Jo into one of those special papoose carrying things that you put on your back, she loved it up there as tall as Dad. I carried the other back pack which held a towel, bucket, spade, bottle of fizzy pop and two disposable nappies "In case of emergency," Dad said and he pulled a disgusted face.

To get to the beach we had to walk through the village, Dad bought a Cornish Pastie from a bakery while Jo and I got in a mess with Mini-Milk ice lollies, we actually saw the Moggie parked down a little side street but no sign of Mum. Dad walked around it, "do you know there's not a spot of rust on the old girl, they just don't make them like this anymore, I might ask Grimesy's Dad how much he wants for her when we get home." Brilliant," I beamed, wiping the sticky mess from my face with my sleeve.

The land dropped away steeply on the other side of the village and a beautiful bay with golden sand lay before us as we descended the hill. I could feel the heat of the sun on the back of my neck as I skipped down the track toward the steps that led to the beach.

This was a good day I thought, a great day, I elevated it from good to great when I realised at this precise moment I would be having double maths with Mrs. Trickett.

Most of the time Mrs. Trickett was quite friendly, but sometimes she became so frustrated with us when we didn't understand something........like long division, she'd literally froth at the mouth and scream at whichever unfortunate child was nearest.

When I was off school recovering from having my tonsils stolen, she became particularly cross with Lenny. He'd failed to do his homework for the fifth time that term,

"Why haven't you done it Mr. Grimes?" she enquired little deposits of froth already appearing in the corners of her mouth.

"I don't know Miss."

"Don't know, don't know, you don't know very much at all do you," she was building up to an explosion.

Dougie tried to distract her from Lenny "Miss, Miss my pens run out," "Run after it boy," she glared at Dougie then returned her beady eyes to Lenny. Poor Lenny, as I said he never knew when to be afraid and by this time he was fighting desperately to hold back an attack of the giggles.

"Wipe that smirk off your face, are you laughing at me?" "Yes Miss," no one can remember what she said next a torrent of words flew from her mouth along with a single tooth on a pink plastic plate.

Which landed on the desk directly in front of Lenny, she was so angry she never even noticed, Lenny stared at the huge black cavity which now became another avenue for froth.

By now the whole class was laughing, except Lenny he was still staring at the black hole. Mrs. Trickett turned to the class and with a huge false smile asked if something was amusing them, now the class beheld the black hole for the first time, the laughing stopped instantly as they too stared into the darkness.

At this point Mr. Lyon came in, curious and concerned about the noise coming from the maths room, he quickly realised what had happened and led Mrs. Trickett out into the corridor.

A moment or two later Mr. Lyon returned and asked the class if anyone had seen Mrs Trickett's tooth, Lenny dutifully put his hand up and pointed to the frothy plate resting on his desk, Mr. Lyon wrapped it in his handkerchief and without speaking left the room. I think poor Mrs. Trickett must have had the rest of the day off, the class had a free lesson and Lenny was a hero.

"Ooooooooaghh!" I cried the gang cry as I ran flat out to the sea, SPLASH! the water crashed against my shins and threw salty water up against my face, I ran out even quicker, it was colder than Mrs. Trickett's glare and just as frothy. Dad and Jo made sand castles while I played in the rock pools, left by the now retreating sea.

"Where does the sea go Dad?"
but he was far too busy, Jo had tried to eat a sand castle and Dad was trying to clean the sand from around her mouth. This was proving to be quite a task, as the sand had stuck to the sticky remains of Jo's Mini Milk ice lolly.

I sat on a large rock my feet dangling in the clear water of the rock pool, small speedy fish came out to look at them, then shot away in fear. I asked if we could go further up the bay and look for caves, "Aye Ray lad, there moit be sum smugglers treasure and the dried up bones of Long John 'imself arrrrr!"

"Ace, will we get to keep it if we find any," Dad just said "Aaaaarr te arrr arrrr," and walked up the beach with a pretend limp, I picked up my stuff and limped after him.

We soon found a large deep cave and after a little exploration decided there was no treasure, so stood at the entrance shouting silly things like "Pooh," and waited for the echo to come back...Pooh...Pooh...Poo...Poo, even Jo joined in.

We moved on, and turned at a great rocky outcrop to find a large portion of the beach completely fenced off, there was a big sign, red with white letters saying DANGER KEEP OUT!

At the foot of the cliff was the strangest sight, a mound of rocks and boulders topped with green turf and the oddest thing, out of one of the clumps of grass was a chimney pot.

"What on earth is it?" "Look above Ray," I followed Dad's pointing finger up the cliff and there about two hundred feet up on a completely unreal angle was a house.

"Woooah, can we climb up and see it." "Don't be silly Ray, that house could fall off the edge and into the sea at any moment."

As he spoke a section of the cliff about the size of a car broke away and crashed down just left of the chimney pot, frightening the seagull that was perched upon it. We watched for a little while longer, but nothing else happened, so we set off back to the camp site.

Dad explained to me all about erosion, in other words how the sea can wear down even solid rock, "They can build rockets to the Moon Ray, but the most powerful thing on the planet is the force of nature, always remember that."

There was a cosy glow from the little gas fire when we got back and the smell of Mum's stew greeted us like an old friend.

We sat in the dining area to eat our meal, and watched the telly which was mounted on the wall, we never got to do that at home so it was a real treat.

And then there it was, the house on an angle on the edge of the cliff. "Dad look,"

"Well I never, that's the house we were telling you about earlier love, turn it up a bit, let's hear what they're saying."

6. Fierce Freddy

Her mousey blonde hair kept blowing across her face and into her mouth as she spoke, the volume rose "............and now it appears that no one will ever know the mysterious and wonderful secrets of the World's greatest explorer, the late Frederick Challenger."

"His house now perched precariously on the edge of this mighty cliff." The camera wobbled and momentarily the lady news reader disappeared from the screen, screams could be heard and I'm sure I heard someone say a rude word.

The camera steady once more showed us a view of the back of her windswept head, she turned white faced, excitement and fear in her voice. I don't know if we caught that on camera viewers but the house just lurched several feet, it must now be only moments away from crashing into the roaring sea below.

The camera zoomed in on the stricken building which was now obviously on an even more ridiculous angle than earlier that day. "Cor, Mum look it's going to fall," but it didn't, the lady continued her report.

"A personal friend to the The King of England, Frederick Challenger disappeared from public life over forty years ago, leaving what came to be known as 'Challenger's Challenge' printed once a year in the New

Years Day edition of The Times.

Many brave young men took up this challenge unsuccessfully and travelled to the corners of the earth to seek out Mr. Challenger, and uncover his secrets and to receive as he put it in The Times *his very special gifts.*

Many of these would be explorers, never returned and we can only wonder what became of them. Of course now we know Frederick Challenger lived here in this house, in this quiet little village known as Abbey. While men from all continents chopped their way through tropical jungles and gave up their lives in hot desserts, he was here, perhaps the last place anyone would expect to find him.

And as we reported on this station some weeks ago, his whereabouts and identity were only discovered when his funeral took place, in a small church two miles up the coast from where we stand, attended only by his close friend and companion Mr. Buckingham.

"We cut now to an interview we filmed with Mr. Buckingham as he was leaving the church that day". It was the same lady news reader looking much calmer than she did today,

"Mr. Buckingham, it must be a very sad day for you."

"Without doubt the saddest day of my life lassie, the country has lost a great man and I have lost a dear, dear friend," he said in a broad Scottish accent.

"Could you tell the viewers anything of his adventures and the many marvellous things he is said to have discovered." "I'm sorry lassie, I'm afraid I cannot, I have sworn a blood oath that I will take his wondrous secrets to my grave." And with that he was gone never to be seen again, not by anyone that is........except myself!

The lady was back on screen her hair now tied back in a pony tail. "Well, we'll be here watching the events from Abbey village as they unfold, we will keep you informed of any developments as they happen, so don't touch that dial, now it's over to John for the regional weather."

"Mum, can we go and watch the house tomorrow." "It might be dangerous Ray and anyway by the look of it, I shouldn't think it will make it through the night." She went on "It was all the talk in the village store, do you know he'd lived here over forty years and no one had ever seen him and Mr. B, oh by the way that's Mr. Buckingham." "He would only come to the village once every three months to pay for the food, which they had delivered by the 'Patels,' lovely couple you know, from Bombay."

"He was known locally as Fierce Freddy, they new his name was Freddy as Mr. B always referred to him as Master Frederick, the 'Fierce' part came from a young man who came in their shop one day in an extremely distressed state." "This chap was a travelling salesman, a very good and therefore very persistent salesman and one day as fate would have it he turned up outside the house on the cliff."

"The huge black wrought iron gates were securely pad locked, so he clambered over ripping the seat of his trousers as he did so."

"This made him all the more determined to sell the occupant 'Super Devloc Double Gazing,' now it was personal."

"He rapped and rapped on the solid oak door and peered through every window," thinking "Mmmmm nice bit of woodworm here, this is going to be so easy." "At last he returned to the front door and with the annoying persistence only a born salesman could have and rapped the solid brass knocker for over half an hour."

"He was just about to give up when all of a sudden the door burst open with a crash that shook the very foundations." "And there he was, a fantastic specimen of a man, standing over six and a half feet tall resplendent in his full khaki jungle wear."

"On his head a pith helmet and below it the most magnificent handle bar moustache you ever saw, nestled under his right arm a double barrel shotgun, fine blue smoke wisping from the barrel as if it had just been used."

"Good afternoon sir, I believe this house presents us with a bit of a challenge!"

"Fierce Freddy looked this small pin striped figure up and down raised a bushy eyebrow and said in a deep strong voice"

"Do you accept the challenge?"

"Oh yes, I do indeed sir, in fact from my preliminary survey I'd say we could save you up to eighty per cent off your heating bills, with our revolutionary UPVc double glazed units."

"The next thing the poor chap knew the two hot smoky barrels of Freddy's shotgun were pressed firmly into his forehead, "Begone Tinker," snarled Freddy his incredibly white teeth flashing from under his huge moustache."

"Most normal human beings would have turned and ran by now but he wasn't a human being, he was a salesman." "But, sir you don't seem to realise how much money you are literally throwing away every year, and if....." "Go while you still can little man," a hint of menace in Freddy's voice. "But really sir..." he was stammering now "I . I . I really think," he never got to finish the sentence,

Freddy's mouth opened as if in slow motion and from it came the most fearsome and frightening roar any one had ever heard."

The salesman now had the good sense to flee for his life, ripping his trousers further on his climb over the gate, he left his car and ran down the hill side exposing the silliest pair of red and white spotted boxer shorts you could imagine. Freddy's roar was still going strong as he reached the outskirts of the village, every villager was out in the street scanning the sky for some type of supersonic jet with an extra loud engine, only the man in the red and white shorts now running through the streets knew that it was really the madman up on the hill.

The Patel's were looking skyward too when the man rushed straight past them into their shop, a moment or two later as the roar died down they went back inside to find this chap half way through a bottle of their best brandy and smoking cigarettes one after another.

"Sorry, sorry," he stammered "I'll pay for everything,"
"You cannot do this," complained Mr. Patel "It is very bad, very bad indeed,"

"Bad, Bad!" cried the salesman "I've never drank or smoked in my life." the salesman then poured out his story to Mr. and Mrs. Patel, who by now were quite sympathetic, Mrs. Patel even sewed up his trousers while Mr. Patel retrieved his car."

Mum finished the story and sat back, quite proud of all the information she'd gathered on her shopping trip.

"I'm sure stories like that get blown out of all proportion, especially in a small village where nothing exciting ever happens," said Dad, but it was too late for me, even if only a fraction of all this was true it was incredible.

What could his very special gifts be? Perhaps his house was full of gold and gems and things that no one in the civilised world had ever seen, and by tomorrow it would be washed out to sea and lost forever.

I decided then and there, before that happened I would, under darkness this very night sneak into Frederick Challengers house and do a bit of exploring for myself!

7. A Cowboy called Worzel

That evening we went to the club house to watch Yukon Bill and the other line dancers in action. A man wearing a black and white frilled cowboy shirt greeted us, "Howdy pardners, welcome to the ho-down," and deposited a cowboy hat on each of our heads, "You all have a good time now, y'here me dears"

His accent was a strange mix of John Wayne and Worzel Gummidge. It was mostly elderly people, I suppose because all the younger people were either at school or work, now the summer holidays were over.

There was only one young couple and they sat in the corner, hardly speaking, just staring at each other and wearing soppy smiles.

"Newlyweds they are, first time they been out of there caravan all week," laughed old Yukon Bill as he came to sit at our table,

"Now then, would any of you nice people like to buy a raffle ticket, we got some crackin' prizes to give away tonight."

Dad bought some and Yukon moved on to the next table,
"Dad, he had crisps stuck in his beard,"

"I know son, perhaps he's saving them for later." Mum laughed and told us not to be disrespectful to the elderly, I couldn't help wondering if Mrs Kilburn ever kept crisps in hers and had a midnight feast in bed when Mr Kilburn was sleeping.

"Just look at that young couple Roy, aren't they sweet?" Dad looked to where Mum was gesturing thought for a second then said "Fancy a game of pool son."

Dad was great at escaping tricky situations, Killer, Death, Doc Harry even Mum. I don't know if Dad thought the newly weds were sweet or not, it was just such an un-Dad-ish thing to say.

"Black ball, side pocket," whack! and the sixth game was over, "That's three each now Ray, lets call it evens, I think the dancing's about to start." As we returned to our seats all manner of cowboy and cowgirl were lining up in readiness.

The man in the black and white frilled shirt was on the stage a microphone in his hand, "Well now everyone are you ready for some country music," they all cheered and whooped their approval.

"Before we git started, we got us some green horns over yonder, from up north," to our horror the whole bunch of cow people turned to look at us and started to clap.

"Are we gonna give 'em a good old south coast welcome or ain't we?" they all whooped and clapped again and two cowboys came and led Mum and Dad onto the dance floor.

This was so funny the look of sheer horror on Dad's face, his dodges had failed him he'd been caught by elderly cowboys.

The man on stage shouted instructions to everybody as the music started, Mum was turning to her left, stomping her foot and clapping her hands with everyone else, Dad was doing something completely different. He almost knocked a lady over completely and in turn she took another dozen cow people with her, eventually they righted themselves and carried on as if nothing had happened.

The frilly black and white cowboy was trying his hardest not to laugh "Tie a rope round that there Mustang before he stomps on your corns," everyone laughed except Dad, he looked even more embarrassed now and seemed to get worse as his country dancing skills had been highlighted.

At the end of the song all the cowboys patted Dad on the back as he made his way back to our table, Mum followed a smile as wide as river across her face, which to her credit she managed to wipe off before sitting down.

"Oh Roy, you were so graceful on the dance floor," she said without a trace of a smile. Dad knew how bad he was, he just pulled his hat down at the front, stuck his thumbs in the belt loops of his jeans and said "D'yer want another Shandy Pilgrim?"

Dad returned from the bar with crisps and drinks, they chatted and laughed, it was like being normal again .... no more staring.

I was the stary one now, I had other things on my mind, I was thinking of the house, what if it had fallen into the sea already, what if it hadn't, would I dare go?

Jo fell asleep on Mum's knee and Dad was yawning, no doubt tired after his long drive and traumatic dance routine, so we made our way wearily back to the caravan.

We all agreed it had been a great first day of our holiday, Jo was making little baby type snoring noises from the travel cot so we all crept quietly to bed.

I lay on the top bunk fully clothed staring at the ceiling and wondering what to do. Earlier that day I had no doubts at all that I should find a way into the house and explore. Now the moment of truth was upon me I thought about the actual reality of it all, it could very easily slip of the edge of the cliff and crash hundreds of feet below with me inside.

"No more Ray Thursday," I said quietly but out loud. Mum and Dad would be really upset, if the sea washed my remains out to sea, no one would ever know what became of me.

Mum might even think I had run away and not even left a note, this would be even more upsetting I decided. I couldn't stare at the ceiling anymore my eyes hurt, I closed them for a second, it was lovely and before I knew it I was dreaming a very odd dream.

It was as if I'd woken up, I looked around my room and remembered I was on holiday, the red numbers on my radio alarm clock seemed to light the whole room and were almost too bright to look at.

I squinted and shaded my eyes with my hand as if staring into the sun, it was midnight.

"Time to go young Mr. Thursday." a voice said, it seemed to be coming from the bunk below me, someone was in my room. I jumped to my feet, hit my head on the ceiling and fell back down onto the mattress.

For a second I forgot the voice coming from the bunk below and rubbed the top of my head waiting for the pain to go, but only for a second. I crept to the edge of my bed, perhaps it was only my imagination, and slowly edged out until I could see below, nothing, I breathed a sigh of relief and relaxed.

Just then a large domed helmet loomed from the shadows followed by a mans head with a moustache which went all the way from one side of

his face to the other. The head was followed by a body which shot athletically out of the bed and stood facing me, his face now level with my own.

I was frozen, I couldn't speak, I couldn't move, I tried to contact Mum or Dad with telepathy it didn't work.

"I do believe you are planning on making a trip to my home this fine evening?" he said in a clipped English accent. I still couldn't move but eventually I did manage to speak, although even I could not believe what I was about to say.

"You're F.F.F.F.F.Frederick Challenger!"
I stammered, "But you're d.d.d d. dead, you can't be here, you just can't be!"

"Calm yourself young Raymond there is no need to be fearful, I am he of whom you speak, or at least I used to be." "So" I replied still trembling "You're a g.g.ghost," it was a statement not a question because that was the only possible explanation.

He looked upwards smiled and said "Yes by George I suppose I am, I'm not quite sure how it all works just yet, but I feel I am on the verge of my greatest adventure yet, it really is quite exciting you know."

"One thing I do know, is that I have this one opportunity to pass a message on to somebody before I move on, and that is why I am here."

"M.M.M. ME." I was stammering again, "why me?"

"Because you my fine young fellow are the last man on this entire planet to consider taking my challenge," then he added "Trust me I've checked, everyone else failed or gave up, once I thought someone had actually made it but it was a snivelling little tinker."

He cleared his throat and stood to attention as if to try and shake off the memory of the double glazing salesman. I had to tell him of my thoughts "You see Mr. Challenger, I'm not altogether sure I still want ...."

He cut me off in mid sentence "Oh yes you do, I can see it in your heart, I pride myself in being a fine judge of character Raymond and you are my last hope, the house will not make it through the night and by tomorrow all will be lost."

"There are many wondrous thing in my home, the likes of which men have never seen and never will see.

"But one item Raymond is more powerful and precious by far, it must not fall into the hands of evil men and yet without an owner it will simply disappear for all eternity." For a moment he looked extremely sad and thoughtful, then he cocked his head to one side as if he was listening to something or someone.

"My time is up now I must bid you farewell and God speed, take care." "Mr. Challenger," "You may call me Frederick, sir," "Frederick sir," "No Raymond just Frederick," "Oh I see, Frederick," as I spoke he began to fade away in front of my very eyes

"Frederick," I was in a state of panic "You still haven't told me what the precious item is that I must find." "Silly me, of course I do apologise, you must find my........." and he was gone.

I couldn't be sure but I thought he said suitcase! And then for a mere instant he was back, causing me to jump in fright "Promise me Raymond, promise me," and he was gone once more. I stared at the spot where he had appeared, then as if in a trance whispered "I promise."

Crash! I was awoken by my window blowing open with tremendous force, the curtains flapping crazily in the wind and then instantly it stopped.

Sticking my head out the window I half expected to see Frederick Challenger, strange there wasn't hamster's breath of wind, it was a lovely still clear night.

An enormous three quarter moon was hanging in the sky like a chinese lantern and I had never seen as many stars in the sky in my whole life,

I'm sure we don't have this many back home.

My dream started to come back to me bit by bit as dreams sometime do, until my memory of it was crystal clear.

Perhaps it was a sign and after all I thought, I had promised.

Within minutes I was making my way through the moonlit streets of Abbey village, heading towards the coast road and Frederick Challenger's house.

8. A Fiery End

It truly was a beautiful clear night, as I crept through the village and crossed the stile to the fields, I found I had no need of my torch. A Moon as large as an Edam cheese, peeked from behind Freddy's house picking out the dark shadowy shapes of the rooftop, with its one remaining wonky chimney.

All around the stars twinkled like Christmas tree lights, it was a special night.....I could feel it, and the excitement rose in my tummy like bubbles in a bottle of lemonade.

By the time I'd reached the great black wrought iron gates, I knew for certain that I had made the right choice. I thought of Frederick Challenger as I crawled damply under the gates and thought of my dream too. If there were such a thing as a ghost he'd probably be watching me right now, getting smartly up from my crawling position I could feel the hairs on the back of my neck standing on end. I span round quickly expecting to see him right behind me, but of course he wasn't.

I was being silly and spooking myself, "Come on Ray don't be a wimp" I thought, and carried onwards. The Moon cast dark shadows behind me as I climbed the stone steps, I could already see the door which was slightly open due to the disturbance. Cautiously I pushed, it didn't budge an inch, I pushed harder this time with both hands against the door, it was no use. I took a run up and threw my shoulder at it, instantly bouncing back with no effect apart from a sharp pain!

This was hopeless, I turned right and walked along the porch, my shoulder still throbbing badly, as I walked along the cock-eyed porch I had to prop myself up with my left arm due to the angle of the house.

Before long I came to a large window, the glass had already shattered and fallen out, my foot made a slight crunching sound as I placed it inside. I was in, although it was extremely hard to balance as the whole room sloped down away from me and I was sliding on the many pieces of broken glass.

I shone my torch on the floor and stepped free, there was better grip on the deep red carpet but I still had to lean backwards to stay upright. Flashing my torch around the room, I at first thought it was empty, then noticed that all the furniture had slid to one end and was piled up against the opposite wall. In the middle and unblocked by clutter was a huge fireplace and all around the room the heads of stuffed animals growled from the walls. Their fierce teeth glistened as the torchlight flashed across their faces.

I decided it would be safer to sit down on my bottom, shuffle my way to the far end of the room and see if there was a way out. Inch by inch I shuffled towards the fireplace, all the time wondering if my weight might upset the fine balance of the house. Every now and again there would be a loud creaking noise, followed by a shower of fine white dust floating down from the ceiling and covering me a ghostly white. Every time it happened I sat quite still curled up in a ball and tried to make my Mrs Kilburn invisible force field.

After a while I gave up on this idea deciding if it couldn't protect me from a furry kiss, it certainly wouldn't protect me from a collapsing house.

The fireplace was right in front of me now, very carefully and very slowly I got to my feet this time standing sideways with my legs apart, as you would if you were sliding on ice. I slid closer and closer until my left hand rested on the cold stone mantlepiece. Above the fire was a vast framed painting, I directed the beam of my torch onto it almost dropping it in absolute shock.

It was a portrait of the late Frederick Challenger, icy cold shivers ran down my back..........he looked exactly as he did in my dream, it was the same face! On the mantlepiece I noticed an object which hadn't rolled off to join the rest of the furniture.

I looked closer, it was a hand gun mounted on a wooden stand, with a small brass plaque on the base. Quickly I wiped the white dust from the plaque and read 'The Ultimate Challenger Pistol.' This would be a great prize to take home, much more exciting than a suitcase. Holding it tightly by the hand grip I pulled, it was stuck as solid as the front door. I grabbed it again, this time by the barrel and pulled with all my might, a creak, it moved but only slightly. I repeated my efforts it moved again, then stuck.

Determined I climbed up onto the huge mantlepiece, planted a foot either side of the wooden mount and gave it my all. Suddenly it happened, the gun barrel swivelled round until it pointed directly to the ceiling, but remained firmly attached to the mount.

Out of breath I sat trying to decide whether to give it one more go, when I noticed the room was gradually becoming lighter, an eerie weird type of light.

From the corner of my right eye I realised the light was coming from the painting. Slowly I arched my neck upwards and gazed in horror. It seemed the painting was alive, I could feel warm breath on the back of my neck oozing from those huge nostrils When I had looked at the painting earlier I was sure the face was kind, now it glared down at me in anger.

A terrible chill came over me and my teeth began to chatter, I didn't have to worry about being cold though, as at that very moment enormous yellow and orange flames leapt from the fireplace beneath my feet. The fire that was dead was now roaring, but worst of all so was Frederick Challenger. From somewhere all around me came awful, humourless laughter, it was so loud I could feel the vibrations of the sound tearing through my body.

I backed up against the painting to escape the flames which were now leaping around my ankles when a voice from somewhere bellowed "Accept the challenge or be doomed." I turned, face to face with Freddy's image, he was no longer angry, he was laughing like a madman. His teeth were whiter than white and seemed to be dripping with clear fluid, but his eyes! They were bulging from their sockets to such an extent it looked like they would explode at any moment. I closed my eyes on this horrible sight and clasped my hands over my ears to drown out the terrible laughter.

There was only one thing for it, I thought for a second of Dad at the sand hills then leapt with all my strength. As I sailed over the flames I cried "Geeeronimoooo" for a moment I thought the flames would melt my trainers, then it was gone and I had landed cat like on the carpet in front of the blazing fire. The laughing stopped and I turned to see the painting glaring down at me, with no hint of emotion.

Another terrifying creak rasped through the house, much louder than before and the angle of the house suddenly shifted. I tried to grip into the fibres of the carpet with my finger nails as the angle steepened forcing me back towards the flames. Mum made me cut them before coming on holiday, fussy as ever, and then I remembered I hadn't left a note!

Now even more determined, I scrambled wildly up the carpet, I was doing it, I was nearly there. Exhausted I had reached the window and was pulling myself up to climb out when my right foot went flying from beneath me, the glass! I lost my grip and was hurtling towards a fiery end. My only chance was to get on my feet and as I neared the fireplace to some how jump back on the mantlepiece.

I stood in the ice sliding position travelling far too fast, more broken glass, my feet went from beneath me and I landed with a thud on my back.

I could feel the immense heat on the soles of my feet, and now my face I had to close my eyes it hurt, I opened them for a split second, I was only feet away, in a moment I would be ashes.

I can actually remember seeing my feet enter the flames, I waited for the pain, it never came.

I whizzed straight through the fireplace and out the other side before the heat could even touch me.

The wind was knocked out of me as I landed in a crumpled heap in a stone recess behind the fire, which was just high enough for me to stand, there was no way out except back through the fire. On the wall to my left I spotted a metal lever sticking out of the stone brickwork, at the top it said ON and at the bottom it said OFF. It was in the 'on' position "Of course" I thought "This is the control for the fire."

I could simply turn it off and get out of this house once and for all, the stupid suitcase can get washed out to sea for all I care. I thrust the lever downwards.

Whooooosh! And downwards was the direction I went, the floor beneath me simply disappeared and I was flying down a chute in complete darkness screaming at the top of my voice.

It turned left, then right, then left again each time I flew up the side of the chute until suddenly the chute ran out! Momentarily I flew through the air before landing on something soft.........I didn't even want to know where I was now?

9. The Beast and the Box

I sat for a while silent and stunned my eyes wide open, I was taking huge gulps of air and wondered how long it would take for my heart to slow down to a normal rate. At least I was alive, I couldn't really believe it but I was still alive, if only for the time being.

My eyes gradually became accustomed to the murky green light, and I could make out that I was in fact in a very large room, the walls were made from huge stone blocks that ran with water, coming from somewhere above the high ceiling. There were no obvious doors or windows, so once again there was no way out.

Without warning a distant rumbling sound began, quiet at first, then loud enough to make my whole body vibrate, it was the sound of great stones grinding together. I just sat where I'd landed, whatever was about to happen, could happen I was far too exhausted to move and it surely couldn't be any worse than I'd already been through, I was wrong!

In the dim light I could make out dark shapes rising up from the ground, great stone pillars, some round, some hexagonal and some square and there seemed to be an object of some kind on top of each one. Precisely in the middle of the room rose a circular pillar, slightly wider and taller than the rest and on it rested a box or at least something box shaped.

All the columns were slowing now and as they finally came to a halt, a blinding beam of light burst over the central pillar, so bright it was almost impossible to look at it.

It did however help to light up the rest of the room, which was even bigger than I first thought, it was only now I realised that I was sitting, and had landed on a colossal bed.

It had great brass fittings at each end and at the top the initials F.C. were built into the design in fancy letters, surely this wasn't Freddy's bedroom I thought, no wonder he hadn't been seen for years.

I lowered myself slowly down, it was quite a drop from the large bed and my feet squelched on the damp floor, it was a lovely feeling and cooled my trainers which surprisingly were still hot from the fire. I stood a while enjoying the moment, apart from my rubber soles I could smell burning, it was me, some of my clothes were still smoking so I rolled on the wet stone floor the backside of my jeans making a hissing sound as I did so!

Next to the bed was an equally huge wooden bedside cabinet, on top stood a copper coloured old fashioned double belled alarm clock which was ticking very loudly in the echo-ey room. I opened the cabinet door expecting perhaps to find a collection of Freddy's socks, but it was empty apart from one piece of folded paper. To my great surprise on the outside of the paper it said 'Raymond Thursday.'

I flipped the sheet over quickly, nervously reading out loud. 'Welcome to my most wondrous bedroom, only the King of England and myself have ever been in this room and seen the wonders it contains, if you are reading this now I offer my heartfelt congratulations on coming this far.'

'Remember only take what is most precious and leave, but be warned when the clock strikes one your time is done, and so will you be if you don't make good your escape!' It was signed Frederick B. Challenger and in brackets underneath 'The World's Greatest Explorer.' P.S. 'Be Careful Lad.'

I looked at my watch and then at the clock, two minutes to one and then I was done! What did it mean I had exactly two minutes before.......before what, I had no idea, I had a sneaking feeling it wouldn't be very enjoyable!

There were strange objects on every pillar and I'm sure they were all wonderful, but unfortunately I never had time to examine them. I made straight for the largest pillar, lit so brightly in the middle of the room and the box that sat upon it. As I strode towards it, my mind raced, was it really what I suspected, if it was then the dream I had earlier that evening was not a dream at all.

Too high, it was too high, even on my tip toes I couldn't see over the top of the pillar, I needed something to stand on and turned to the smaller pillar only a couple of feet high immediately behind me. On it sat the huge pith helmet that Freddy always wore, grabbing it quickly I placed it at the bottom of the large pillar.

It seemed to act as some kind of trigger because as soon as I lifted the hat from its resting place a distant rumbling started and I was convinced I just felt a large spot of rain land on my head!

I glanced at my watch one minute left, no time to waste, I jumped on the hat but I still couldn't see the box. Standing on the tip toes of my right leg only and holding on to the ledge of the pillar with my left hand I could feel the side of the box. I gave it one almighty push and it flew off the edge, at the same time I toppled off the helmet and crashed to the floor. And very fortunate it was that I did, the box must have been another trigger for a trap, as I lay on the floor still dazed five spears whizzed over me and embedded themselves into the stone wall with a sickening thud. Two went either side of the pillar and the other three went over the top at different heights, had I been standing, one of them would have surely hit me.

There was no time to think of what might have been, I quickly scrambled around to the other side of the pillar to gather my prize.

It lay there on the damp floor, big raindrops spotting on its shiny brown leather, for it was raining now and I finally realised my dream was not a dream at all and that's why the painting looked like the Freddy I'd spoke to that night.

But most of all that was why I was now staring down at a small brown leather suitcase!

It certainly didn't look much, slightly battered and covered in travel labels from many different countries, what did he call it his "wonderful suitcase" and that this above all else must be saved.

The rain was becoming torrential, I couldn't see the ceiling at all just a mass of black clouds, to my right a bolt of fork lightning hit the brass bed head and totally lit up the room for an instant.

Thunder rumbled, the sound was quite deafening and then above it all a tremendous ringing, the alarm clock!

When I turned to look in the direction of the bedside cabinet I could see the clock vibrating madly, my time was up, I was done! I clasped the small suitcase to my chest and was staring wildly around the room when I heard a familiar noise.

Above the roar of the storm I could hear once more the sound of stone against stone, it seemed to be coming from the far end of the room.

Several stones in the wall were moving in different directions like a puzzle and creating a doorway, perhaps this was my way out. I grabbed my case and galloped through about three inches of rain water towards my escape route.

I'd survived the dangers, passed the tests, got the suitcase and now the room was showing me a way out, for the first time I allowed myself a smile, patted the suitcase and said "Come on we're getting out of here."

With new hope I sploshed forwards and then stopped dead in my tracks! Somebody was sploshing towards me coming from the darkness on the other side of the door.

"Hello, is anybody there, I've got the suitcase, can I go home now?" no reply just the splosh, splosh, splosh growing louder and louder. "Hello, can you hear me, is this the way out?"

I was just tilting my head to listen for an answer when I saw a huge black shape in the darkness, instinctively I took several steps back as the shadowy shape emerged from the doorway.

I'd seen one once before, at the Zoo, a Bengal Tiger!

It saw me, "Nice pussy," I said stupidly, as it fixed me with it's cold stare, a stare that seemed to penetrate to my bones until I felt my body freeze in panic. It rolled it's mighty head and growled a blood curdling growl, at least this snapped me out of my temporary frozen state and I began to back up very slowly, never taking my eyes of the huge beast.

As I moved cautiously back it seemed to lower itself as if ready to pounce and moved with me, maintaining the same distance between us. I couldn't breathe, my mouth had dried up completely and I had no spit left.

Thud! I'd backed right into the large pillar, my legs were wobbly and I slid down into a sitting position the suitcase firmly clasped against my chest, the only thing between myself and the snarling tiger. There was nowhere to run and even if there were, my legs would not take me, this was definitely the end, and I hadn't left Mum a note.

"Dear Mum, sorry I'm not in my bed this morning I went out last night and was eaten by a Tiger, Your Loving Son, Raymond," that would have made things much better I thought.

It crouched, ready to leap and roared, I shut my eyes tight all I could hear was the tiger roaring and then above even that an incredibly loud cracking. Everything moved, the house had shifted violently again, gallons and gallons of rainwater, the tiger and myself were now all rushing towards the doorway at the far end of the room.

Sticking out my right arm I managed to grab one of the smaller pillars, clambered around it and got my feet on the other side, I leaned over the top to see the tiger sink its terrifying claws into the very stone and begin to edge its way towards me once more, still intent on its next meal in other words Ray Thursday.

The whole room was shaking terribly, large pieces of stone crashing down into the torrent of water, the noise was terrifying, it was like the whole house was screaming in agony. The floor itself began to break up, but still the beast clawed its way closer and closer, there was a deafening crack and a massive crevasse appeared at the far end of the room, perhaps ten feet wide.

It shot towards us like a bolt of lightning, the tiger was closer than ever, only inches from my face, no doubt wondering what I would taste like, when suddenly the earth below swallowed him up and he was gone.

With the speed of an express train the gaping hole headed in my direction, without thinking I hurled myself to the left and thankfully it just missed swallowing me too! I rolled onto my belly and found myself looking down into the blackness of the crevasse.

Pushing myself back from the edge I rested my head momentarily on my arms, I had to move, I had to head for the doorway it was my only hope. I lifted my head wearily and just as I did two huge paws landed either side of my face quickly followed by the head of the great and now extremely angry tiger. Without thinking I swung my left arm and hit him hard on the side of his face with the suitcase and he disappeared once more into the blackness, roaring his contempt as he fell.

For perhaps the first time I agreed with Freddy, this truly was a wonderful suitcase. Jumping to my feet I ran towards the doorway nearly slipping on several occasions, I wasn't about to wait for Mr. Tiger to make a third appearance.

It was steep now the house had moved and torrents of water were gushing through the doorway. I gushed with it and was consumed by the darkness, but continued to run flat out, almost immediately I could see light at the end of the long corridor. New energy coursed through my body and I ran like the wind, darkness was ending it was definitely getting lighter, the room at the end was lit so bright it had to be safe.

The dark ended and I burst fearlessly into the bright room, my feet, where were my feet, I couldn't feel them!

With great horror I realised it was not a brightly lit room, I had run down a long corridor straight out of the side of the cliff just below Freddy's house, the light was the moon and now I was falling, falling towards the rocks on the beach below.

Every muscle in my body tensed and I waved my arms as if trying to fly, I should have written Mum a note! Instead I screamed at the top of my voice HELP!

No sooner had I done so then I felt a tug on my right arm, I looked up and to my amazement saw that a parachute in the colours of the Union Jack had opened from the suitcase and I was floating safely to earth.

I grabbed the handle of the suitcase with both hands and as I turned to my left saw a very strange sight, Freddy's house was passing me on the way down, it didn't make a sound until it hit the rocks below, when it sent up a huge cloud of dust, which I floated gently through and onto the beach.

I actually landed with a splash in a rock pool, the splash was followed by a swishing sound and I looked down to see the parachute whizzing back into the suitcase from wherever it had come from.

A cold wave washed over the backs of my legs bringing me back very much to reality and I gazed up to where the house once stood, now there were only cliffs.

Tired, extremely wet, extremely cold, but alive, I stepped out of the pool onto the sand, I had the wonderful suitcase. I raised it to the moon and let out the gang cry, "Oooooooooaaagh!"

10. Caught in the Act

I stumbled wearily through the waves towards the steep stone steps, which led back up to the village. A soft squelching sound came from my soggy trainer as I planted it on the first step and gazed upwards, wondering if I had enough strength left to get to the top.

Out of the darkness to my right came a voice "Congratulations young laddie, allow me to introduce myself, I am Mr. Buckingham an associate of Mr. Challenger," I remembered him from the television news programme.

The fact that someone came out of the shadows at this hour didn't take me aback at all, I'd already been through so much, I simply took it in my stride and replied "Hi, I'm Ray Thursday." "Indeed you are, Indeed you are Mr. Thursday," he chirruped grabbing my free hand and shaking it vigorously, "I cannot tell you how pleased I am to see you, and that you actually made it with Mr. C's wonderful suitcase."

With a hint of sadness he added "It's such a shame Mr. C. couldn't have been here to see it, he would have been so pleased that someone finally came along to carry on his work, he'd waited so long you know."

I was far too tired, battered and bruised to tell Mr. Buckingham of my dream, so just said "I think he knows," he looked at me curiously for a moment, I smiled he smiled right back at me and said "Aye laddie, he probably does."

"Anyway" I said "I must be off before Mum and Dad miss me, but what exactly is so wonderful about this suitcase, apart from the fact it's got a Union Jack parachute inside." "What am I thinking of, babbling on like an old fool, that is precisely why I am here," he reached inside his jacket and handed me a sealed letter, simply marked 'My Successor.'

"This was written by the great man himself some forty years ago, contained within are instructions on how to use the suitcase, read them carefully Raymond and remember with the suitcase comes great responsibility."

I stared at the words trying to take in exactly what they meant, "I don't understand, what responsibility, what am I supposed to do?" But he'd gone, disappeared once more mysteriously into the darkness. In the distance I faintly heard his broad Scots accent "Don't worry Ray laddie, just do what's right and all will be well."

I stuffed the letter in my back pocket and squelched up the steps. When I got back to our caravan, I stripped down to my trainers and shorts and hung my sodden, smoky clothes on the rotary washing line outside. Now all I had to do was tip toe into the caravan, get into bed and no one would be any the wiser, everything was going as planned, I was a few short steps from my bedroom door when the lights went on!

It was Dad, I don't know which of us looked the more shocked, probably him, I must have been quite a sight and that's probably why it took a whole minute for him to finally speak. "Raymond Thursday, what on earth have you been up to!" I knew he was angry as he called me by my full name, I didn't know what to say so just stood there dripping on the carpet. "Just look at you, your soaked to the skin and your teeth are chattering, where have you been?"

"On the beach" I wasn't really lying,
"And where did you get that old suitcase from?"

"I found it," I was now.
Dad muttered something under his breath, as he threw his large coat around me, and ran me a hot bath.

"Right, in you go or you'll catch pneumonia, we'll talk when you come out of the bath."

Like most young boys having a bath wasn't exactly my favourite past time, but this was one of the greatest experiences of my young life, the aches and pains seemed to soak away into the soapy water, which was rapidly turning a dark-ish shade of grey and I began to relax.

I had no idea what questions Dad would throw at me, so I decided just to try and tell the truth. When I emerged steaming and pink in my best 'tonsils' pyjamas, a big mug of hot chocolate and Dad were waiting for me.

"Thanks Dad," "Never mind thanks Dad," he said quietly more worried than angry, "What have you been doing on the beach until this hour, you could have been washed out to sea!"

"I wanted to see the house one more time before it disappeared and I actually saw it fall off the cliff," this didn't seem to help Dad's mood at all. "You silly, silly boy, you could have been killed, what would your Mother have said," it struck me as funny, we were both concerned about what Mum would have said if something terrible had happened, not particularly what the actual terrible thing was.

"I'm sorry Dad, I meant to leave a note, I'll apologise to her in the morning."

"You'll do no such thing, she'd be frantic, we'll keep this little escapade between ourselves or it will spoil the whole holiday."

"And what's this old piece of junk you've brought home with you?"

"It's a suitcase Dad, I think it belonged to Fierce Freddy."

"I don't think the world's greatest explorer would be travelling the globe with a tatty old suitcase like that Ray."

He called me Ray, he was calming down and I still hadn't really lied, I just hadn't told the whole truth and even if I did I thought, he would never have believed me and I'd be in worse trouble for telling a Lenny-type tall story.

My eyes were heavy, the warmth of the bath and the hot chocolate had finished me off. Dad picked me up in a fireman's lift, he hadn't done that for years, carried me into the bedroom and deposited me on the top bunk.

"Ray, why have you still got that old suitcase in your hand," I didn't open my eyes "Don't know, Dad..........can I keep it?"

"We'll see," he said "We'll see," he always said that, "Go to sleep now," I did before he finished the sentence.

11. Open Sesame, or not as the 'Case' may be!

I slept like a log, but didn't wake up in the fireplace as Dad often joked. I was actually awoken by a thump, I still had the handle of the suitcase firmly grasped in my hand and when I moved in my sleep, gave myself a right good whack on the head with it.

In a certain amount of pain I slowly managed to sit up in bed, rubbed the sleep from my eyes and stretched my aching limbs. Dad must have been busy during the night as all my clothes had been washed, dried and were now folded neatly on the chair by my bed. I set the suitcase on my lap and flicked the catches, they never moved and I hurt my thumbs, it was locked, great!

Good old Dad, I smiled as I hitched up my trousers, now Mum would never know, he'd got me off the hook. I grabbed the suitcase and threw it under the lower bunk, in case Mum saw it. I would have to say I found it, on the beach perhaps, maybe she wouldn't even ask and then I wouldn't have to lie.

Only Mum was in the caravan when I emerged from my room, "Morning Mum," "Morning!" she replied,

"It's almost the afternoon, I thought you were going to sleep the whole day, what would you like for your breakfast love?"

"Just some cereal please Mum, where's Dad and Jo?"

"Dad's took the Moggie to the garage to fill her up with petrol, we're off to Gridlington-on-Sea today, there's a fun fair and donkey rides for Jo."

"Great" I replied, dribbling milk all the way down my chin and back into the bowl. She went on "You'll never guess what happened while you've been sleeping," "What?" I said hoping it wasn't anything to do with me and dribbling even more than before, this time sending a small river of milk down my chin, neck, chest and coming to rest in a little reservoir which was my belly button.

"Well you know that house on the cliff the one we saw on television last night," "Yeah,"

"Its not there any more, sometime during the night the cliff side must have collapsed and now because there was a high tide last night, there are only a few bits of rubble left at the base of the cliff."

"Oh wow, really!"

I tried to sound sincere and may have overdone it slightly, she looked at me for a moment and carried on, "Yes really, but that isn't the best of it!" she was toying with me now and trying to keep me in suspense,

"The really, really strange thing is that trapped by it's tail under the rubble was a fully grown lion, or it might have been a tiger, one or the other,"

"No way!"

"Oh yes, apparently it was so exhausted the poor thing could barely stand, so the police put in the back of their car and took it to the local zoo."

"Can you imagine Raymond, walking along the beach and bumping into a fully grown man eating lion or tiger, ooooh it makes me shiver just thinking about it."

"It was old Yukon Bill that told your Dad this morning, he found it when he was walking his dog, and now his dog won't come out of his cabin, I bet it's the last time he'll be chasing cats!"

"The zoo are going to send him and his dog a letter of thanks and they've named it 'Bill' in his honour!" A letter, I thought, a letter, something about a letter, a feeling of dread suddenly came over me as I remembered my letter!

"Are you alright Raymond, you've gone quite pale?"

"Eh...what....sorry Mum what did you say?"

The letter Mr. Buckingham had given me, the instructions for the suitcase, it was in the back pocket of my jeans. Mum always checked my pockets before she washed them, ever since I had a full packet of bubble

48

gum in my school trousers, when she ironed them it ooozed out and stuck to the iron, I was in so much trouble.

Did Dad check my pockets, did he find the letter or did it get washed with my jeans?

I couldn't decide which would be worse.

My heart sank as I slowly slid my hand into my back pocket and felt something resembling cardboard. "Just going to clean my teeth Mum," "Good lad."

I locked the bathroom door and took the compressed envelope out of my pocket, the words 'My Successor' had washed away completely leaving only a light blue stain, I prayed the writing inside was in better condition. It began to break up as I unfolded it, there was what seemed to be just one sheet of paper inside, small drops of sweat rolled down my forehead as I peeled it apart as slowly as possible, I could make out some words, Bang! Bang! I almost jumped through the ceiling!

"I'm just off to the camp shop Raymond I'll only be two minutes," Mum said knocking on the door as she spoke and almost killing her only son at the same time. I waited to hear the door close and rushed out and plugged the travel iron in, I could flatten the letter and dry it at the same time.

It hissed like a snake and a small puff of steam rose as I placed it gently on the letter, it seemed to be working, the writing wasn't totally clear but I could make most of it out. At the top it said in big capital letters, 'SUITCASE INSTRUCTIONS'

The rest of the letter was written in proper handwriting, which would be a little harder to read, I saw the Moggie pull up outside, quickly I cleared everything away and put the letter under my mattress.

By the time Dad had got Jo out of the car I was sitting down finishing my breakfast, "Hi Dad," he winked at me,

"Where's your Mum?" "Shop."

"Here" he said and passed me this weeks edition of The Beano,

"Or great, thanks Dad."

"Just make sure you're in bed reading it tonight and not out for a midnight stroll on the beach, d'yer hear me Ray."

"Yes Dad, I won't, I'm sorry."

No more was said of the matter and we had a great day at Gridlington, the fun fair was brilliant, I got all the little men down on the rifles, three times in a row and the man gave me a massive multi-coloured candy floss as a prize, later I had a hot dog and a huge red see through lolly that was almost as big as my face.

I felt a little sick on a ride called 'The Twister' but managed to keep everything down, I was very proud of myself and thought it a great achievement.

Later we did some shopping and in a little second hand book shop, I spotted a book called Great Explorers of the 20th Century, I pleaded with Mum to buy it for me and she gladly did so.

"Nice to see you're taking an interest in reading something apart from your comics Raymond," she said patting me on the head, the man in the bookshop smiled, I was embarrassed but still managed to thank her.

I hoped there might be something on Freddy in it, also I could say I was going to read in my bedroom that evening, when really I would be trying to figure out what the suitcase instructions were.

But to tell you the truth I forgot all about the book for the rest of the holiday. Later that evening, I made my excuses and said I was going to read in my bedroom. Lying on the top bunk I carefully spread the sheet of paper out in front of me, I had a drawing pad, a pen and I began to copy down what I thought was written.

After the title, was a complete paragraph of text that was totally unreadable and below that was a list in slightly larger letters, most of this I could read. I picked up my pen and wrote 'The List' and underlined it twice, to show it's importance. I left a space and then I wrote this,

1) T_ o__n s__ply _ay _our __m_ _a_____d_.
2) When jumping close ___ door __hind you.
3) _____ Soap only w__ks for 30 __nutes.
4) Toothpaste is __r _leanin_ _eeth, _ery i__ort__t.
5) C__t _anger __es in _he di__ct_on y__ p__l.

I copied this list out ten times and tried many different letters in the blank spaces, Mum came in with a drink for me and I pretended I was drawing, as soon as she was gone, I ripped out a fresh page and wrote my finished but still incomplete list.

1) To open simply say _our __m_ _a_____d_.
2) When jumping close the door behind you.
3) _____ Soap only works for 30 minutes.
4) Toothpaste is for cleaning teeth, very important.
5) Coat hanger goes in the direction you pull.

I was extremely pleased with myself, I had nearly all the missing letters, yet at the same time I was very disappointed, none of it seemed wonderful or exciting and most of it made no sense at all.

I still couldn't open the suitcase, clue one was the most unreadable and that seemed to be the one I needed, I had to say something before it would open but the letters and gaps made no sense. I tried a few sayings, "Open Sesame," "Open Suitcase," "Open Wonderful Suitcase," nothing happened and I felt stupid talking to it.

I was losing patience with the whole thing, so went to the kitchen and sneaked a bread knife up my sleeve, "I'll open you now," I thought "Whether you like it or not." I placed the knife behind one of the catches and tried to lever it open, no good, then I tried to slide the knife in between the gaps of the leather, it was has if it was made of solid steel.

I threw it in sheer frustration, back under the lower bunk and that's where it stayed for the rest of my holiday, without giving it a single thought.

I never knew then that the second hand book Mum had bought me, would be the key to unlocking its secrets, and so the following week I made one last effort.

12. Stupid Suitcase!

The holiday was great and just what Mum and Dad needed, the little Moggie got us home safely and Dad decided to buy it from Lenny's Dad when we got home.

After a few days things got back to how they were, Dad was restless all the time, he'd had no luck with any of the jobs he'd written for and I could see he wasn't happy. I overheard him talking to Mum about possibly moving away again, I couldn't bear the thought of this, I'd never see my friends again! Surely there was something I could do, but what?

I must admit, I did for a short time think the so-called wonderful suitcase may have been the answer to all our problems. Now I thought the best use that could be made of it was to pack my clothes in, when we have to move away from everything and everyone we know, it was very depressing.

Looking back I wasn't sure it was worth all the effort, almost burnt alive, killed by deadly spears and eaten by a hungry tiger, and now all it did was sit on the shelf in my bedroom.

It did look very colourful and I suppose it was a souvenir of one of the most thrilling nights of my entire life, but I felt I'd been cheated. I'd took the challenge, passed the tests and then I was robbed by washing powder,

I felt a failure, I felt Frederick Challenger laughing at me.

That afternoon we were sat in the classroom when Mr. Lyon came in and whispered something to Mrs. Trickett. "Alright children settle down now," she yelled above the noise "Today you may all go home early, put your books away and leave the school in an orderly manner, no running or it will be double detention tomorrow, this means you Leonard!"

"Yes Miss" Lenny said sheepishly then turned to me "Come on Ray a few of us are going to play at the docks, there's a new boat that's come in,"

"Sorry Lenny I can't today, I've got something I have to do."

I'd made my mind up to have one last attempt to open the stupid suitcase, as I now called it.

We heard on the way out of the main door, that there was a gas leak in the science lab and that's why we had to be sent home, it turned out later that someone in the fourth year had let off a stink bomb.

"Wouldn't it be ace if the whole place blew up," said Dougie "No more school," at one time I would have agreed but I'd seen what having no job was doing to Dad.

Out of the kitchen window I could see Dad digging over the same patch of earth in the back garden, it made me sad, Mum and Jo were out so I grabbed the toolbox and struggled upstairs, dropping it on my bedroom floor and making a great thudding sound.

Quickly I ran to Dad's room and peered from behind the curtains, still digging, he hadn't heard a thing, that was good, as I was about to make some serious noise.

I set the suitcase on the floor and took out the electric drill, nervously I gently squeezed the trigger, it whirred into life, making me jump in fright. I checked on Dad, still digging, I picked up the drill again aimed it at one of the metal clasps and drilled until my fingers began to hurt.

The whirring stopped as I released my fingers, expectantly I picked up the suitcase and examined the clasp. Unbelievably there wasn't so much as a scratch on it.

I decided to drill a hole right through the leather, concentrating I held the drill in the same position for at least five minutes, it was impossible to do it any longer as smoke was beginning to rise from the drill bit and it was glowing red hot.

I hurriedly wafted the smoke away with my hand to examine the damage, there was none!

I tried a big hammer, a chisel, a saw, and by now the palm of my right hand was red and small blisters were beginning to appear, I couldn't do any more, I hated to admit it but I felt like crying.

I didn't, instead I kicked the stupid suitcase around the room, each time calling it stupid! After returning Dad's toolbox I picked up the small brown leather case that had caused me so much trouble and put it outside in the dustbin, slamming the metal lid down on it aggressively, once more and finally saying out loud "Stupid suitcase!"   I couldn't sleep, it was one of those nights like Christmas Eve or the night before our holiday, under torchlight I read my comic, I'd read it before and looked for something else.

Still lying on my bedside cabinet was the book Mum had bought on holiday, out of curiosity I went straight to the back to see if Freddy had a mention, yes there he was on page 75 and page 117. Flicking to page 75 there was a black and white photograph of Freddy, his huge moustache dominating the picture, and underneath a small paragraph written by fellow explorer Stanley Kenyon.

He obviously had a very low opinion of Freddy and couldn't understand what all the fuss was about, or why he should even be mentioned in a book like this. "After all," he said "What did the great Frederick Challenger ever achieve, what did he actually discover, nothing of importance like Raleigh's potatoes or Columbus's New World."

"For the very life of me I cannot understand why the much respected late King declared him the world's greatest explorer, the mere notion of it is ludicrous and an insult to the great men who went before him."

Not a happy chappie, I thought and moved on to page 117, here was an old photograph of Freddy in some distant jungle surrounded by local tribesmen and in his left hand, it was, it must be, the suitcase! There it was as clear as day the stupid suitcase that was now outside in our dustbin. The man who wrote this piece was hoping to write a book about the life of Freddy and his many adventures.

Unfortunately he couldn't find any information about him anywhere, after numerous failed attempts he at last managed to gain audience with the ageing King, but this also proved fruitless.

The only thing the old King would say was "Let me assure you young man, Frederick is without doubt the world's greatest explorer, he has shown me things that the world is not yet ready for, and has been to places that no man of his generation has ever been or ever will." The writer was even more curious now and decided to set off and track Challenger down himself, eventually after five long years, he found him.

Deep in the Amazon Rain Forest an indian hunting party said they had seen the man he was looking for, the locals referred to him as the giant caterpillar man because of his furry moustache.

They pointed him in the right direction and after several hours of slogging and cutting through dense vegetation he came to a clearing and standing in the middle wearing his huge pith helmet was Frederick Challenger.

The writer wasn't about to let him slip away into the forest, so crept quietly within a few feet of Challenger, who was still standing with his back to him.

It was at this moment that Freddy suddenly spoke out loud in strange language, a language that no one had ever heard before, or since. "Kir Red Erf Regnel Ahc," and with that he jumped into the air and on landing was seemingly swallowed up by the very earth beneath his feet!

I slammed the book closed, my eyes wide and watering a feeling of tremendous excitement washing over my entire body.

This was it, this was the answer to instruction number one, 'To open simply say our..a.........' and then the magic words in the strange language.

I immediately retrieved the suitcase from the dustbin, scraping food from its battered brown leather and apologising to it as I climbed the stairs back to my room.

Standing the case in front of me I took the book and trembling slightly read out loud the magic words, "Kir Red Erf Regnel Ahc," I closed my eyes tight and held my breath.......... breathing again I opened my right eye slightly and gazed down at the suitcase.

And there it stood exactly as it was before, still closed, still locked, still stupid! I kicked it harder than ever, hurting my foot. Hopping around on one foot I cursed the case and Freddy and the book and the strange foreign language, but most of all I cursed myself for being so gullible and backwards, to believe such a stupid story.

"Yep Ray, you must be stupid with a capital 'S' and backwards with a capital 'B', even Lenny wouldn't have believed any of this, backwards, backwards, backwards!" I thought to myself.

Then I said out loud, but quietly in a whisper "Backwards" and ran over to the book, found the page and read the foreign words out loud, but this time backwards.

It read, as you can read for yourself 'CHA LENGER FRE DER RIK,' it wasn't spelt correctly, but I suppose this is what the writer heard, it was Freddy's name backwards.

Books and bits of paper flew over my shoulder as I searched through my drawers for the pad, the one I'd wrote the list on while on holiday. Got it, I read instruction number one, 'to open simply say _our __m_ _a____d_,' my pen flew across the blanks it was now complete, and it said 'to open simply say your name backwards.'

I wrote out in big capital letters RAYMOND THURSDAY and then underneath in the easiest way to actually say I wrote YAD SRUHT DNOM YAR.

Several times I practiced saying it in my head, until I was ready and once more placed the suitcase on the floor,

"Ready Ray," I said to myself and I cleared my throat.

13. Thursday's Child has far to Go

"Yad Sruht Dnom Yar!" immediately there was a small mechanical whirring sound, very quiet at first and then gradually growing louder, it was as if many little wheels and cogs were turning and falling into place, then Snap! it stopped and the two catches opened simultaneously.

I bent down very slowly to lift the lid but it was already rising to meet me, a soft golden light full of twinkley bits like glitter, coming from somewhere within, I took a small step back. It was now fully open and gradually the golden light faded away, until once more it looked like an ordinary suitcase.

I dropped down onto my knees, partly to have a closer look and partly because my legs had gone quite wobbly.

I'd thought a lot about what the suitcase might contain, gold, diamonds, rubies, treasure from some distant land or perhaps a map, a map that could lead me to the places that no man apart from Freddy had ever been to.

I slowly crawled closer, there were some items of clothing, sand coloured trousers and shirt, a matching floppy canvas hat, two pairs of socks, brown boots the type you would use for walking, a leather belt, a canteen full of water. I took them all out one by one and placed them neatly on the bedroom floor beside me.

All that was now left in the suitcase was a toothbrush and mmmmmm. mint toothpaste, an old black twisted wire and wood coat hanger and a large block of what looked like soap.

I say it looked like soap, I wasn't really sure if it was, it had no smell whatsoever and was kind of a see-through purple colour, when I held it to the light it almost disappeared from sight, weird, I thought and then noticed stamped into the soap the initials F.C. Frederick Challenger.

This must be the 'something' soap that only lasts for thirty minutes, I'd find out quite soon what the 'something' was.

Over all I was quite disappointed with the suitcase's contents, there was nothing exciting, or of any real value, perhaps I'd missed something. My hands ran round the inside of the suitcase checking for any hidden panels, nothing, it was only then that I noticed the strange material lining of the case.

It was a light cream silky material with very fine brown print, the pattern was made up of lots of little circles growing gradually smaller and smaller, the circles seemed to go on forever and after staring at it for a while, it made me feel slightly dizzy. It was as if the pattern was slowly pulling me towards it, like some kind of visual magnet, turning away I shook my head to clear it of the dizziness and decided to try on the clothes.

Everything fit perfectly even the boots, I clipped the canteen of water onto the brown leather belt and placed the floppy hat on my head "There done" I said as I stared at myself in the dresser mirror.

"Boy do I look silly," I looked like a miniature Freddy apart from a different hat and of course no moustache, I leant closer and checked my upper lip, no it would be years before I could grow one of them, even if I wanted one.

I spoke to my reflected image "Hello there, I'm Raymond Thursday the world's smallest explorer," "Oh yes, fought off a tiger you know, gave it a jolly good whack with my suitcase, haw haw haw," I said copying Freddy's extremely posh accent.

My watch gave out a small beep, as it did on the hour, "Blimey and gosh, it's two o'clock in the morning old bean, you must excuse me I should have retired hours ago haw haw haw," with that I bid myself good night and crawled into bed.

I was looking forward to tomorrow, not only was it Saturday, so no school, but Lenny was staying over, because his Mum and Dad were going to a party.

Lenny called for me just after lunch and we walked to the local shops to get the things that were necessary for a successful sleep-over, ding dong went the bell as we entered Jonesy's.

Mrs. Jones's shop was wonderful, it was crammed to the ceiling with every possible kind of fizzy drink and sweets you could imagine, Dad said it had hardly changed since he was a lad when Mrs Jones's Mother had it.

Lenny and I were regulars and Mrs. Jones new us both well, "Hello boys, and what are you two up to today?" she asked as if to suggest we were up to no good, but only in fun.

"We're having a sleep-over at Ray's house tonight, so we need lots of goodies, fizzy drinks and two scary video's please,"

I would have preferred action films or comedies but Lenny liked to get scared and then tell ghost stories, we very rarely got any sleep when he stayed over.

That evening I decided to tell Lenny of my adventure while on holiday, he just smiled and said "That's a good one Ray, a very good one, I'd be proud of it myself,

"No honestly, it's true, every word of it," I said as I pulled out from under my bed, the suitcase.

"You're not going to tell me that's the wonderful suitcase are you, the worlds greatest explorer took that old thing with him everywhere!"

"That's exactly what Dad said the night he caught me bringing it back to the caravan," "Come off it Ray, this is worse than my peanut butter story."

"A-ha" I yelled, "so it was just a story,"

"Course it was Ray, I never thought you believed it, I just did it to wind the others up, I can't believe you actually believed me,"

"I didn't, honest, just checking that's all."

I placed the suitcase on the floor in front of us, "Just watch this then," and I said my name backwards

"Yad Sruht Dnom Yar,"

"Hey, what are you on about now,"

"Shuuush, just listen Lenny, listen." I saw Lenny's eyebrows raise, until I thought they might go right over the back of his head and join his neck, as the lid moved slowly to fully open and the golden glow once more faded, Lenny for the first time in his life was speechless.

I had to nudge him on the shoulder to get him working again, "Well, what do you say now peanut butter man?"

"That's neat Ray, that's really neat, I don't know how you did it,"
"Leonard!" I was getting cross with him now,
 "I didn't do anything, the suitcase does it by itself."
"If it's so special, then why is it filled with some of your old clothes?" I
gave up, "Want to watch 'The Beast from Mars' now?"
 "Okay" and we settled down for our first film of the evening. After
about half an hour there was a particularly blood thirsty bit, which I
wasn't altogether sure I wanted to watch, "I'll nip down and get the drinks
from the fridge, shall I?" but I couldn't drag my eyes away from the
screen.
 The Beast from Mars's head filled the entire screen, he was chomping
down on several American soldiers, who were screaming in agony.
 "That'll teach 'em," said Lenny who was sitting behind me, I was
puzzled "Teach who, what?"
"Teach 'em to ruin our crunchy peanut butter," we both laughed,
I stood, "Well?"
 "Well, what?"
"Well do you want me to get your drink or not,"
 "Yeah okay, Ray keep your hair on, your not frightened are you, you
don't think the Beast from Mars is coming to gobble you up."
 "Ha ha, very funny," I watched a bit more to prove him wrong, the
Beast had spotted tanks and jet planes heading his way, a missile

exploded against his ginormous scaly shoulder, and he let out a terrible roar.

At this precise moment, and unknown to me Lenny had picked up a long cardboard tube, that had once held one of my bedroom posters, one end was placed on his mouth while the other was hovering just next to my right ear.

He picked his moment carefully and as the Beast from Mars opened his mouth to let out an even more terrifying roar than before, so too did Lenny.

The sound hit my ear, sending a tingling shiver through it, which then proceeded to travel the length of my body, finally reaching my feet.

I leapt several feet in the air, I could hear Lenny, now roaring with laughter as I landed slap bang in the middle of the opened suitcase. But I never landed, for what seemed like a whole minute I was plunged into total darkness and total silence.

Then came a whooshing noise, as I was thrown into a blinding light and landed firmly on my backside in the snow, and this brings me to the start of my story, to the present time or maybe the past, I don't know which.

But here I am, being marched across this snow covered field, with a sword every now and again prodding me in the back and a whole troop of Roman soldiers behind me.

And if all that wasn't bad enough, I was still wearing my pyjamas and slippers!

14. Maximus Nasticus

"Faster boy, or you'll feel my steel!" He prodded me again harder than before and laughed, it was difficult to keep up the pace, my legs were much smaller than theirs and by now my slippers were soaking.

My feet hurt terribly, with the intense cold and I didn't think I could go on much longer, perhaps when Lenny made me jump I fell on landing, perhaps I'm unconscious or in a coma, anything would be better than this.

The Centurion raised his right arm and the soldiers came to a halt, I stopped too, "Make camp!" shouted farty breath, I sat on my suitcase rubbing my feet, trying to get some feeling and warmth back into them.

The soldiers were busy making a camp, they were extremely efficient and within five minutes there was a circle of small white tents, and a large fire burning in the middle.

The Centurion with the breath, strode up to me, grabbed me by the back of my pyjama collar and dragged me within the circle, dumping me face down in the snow, one of the soldiers had just finished hammering a huge metal stake into the frozen earth and I was attached to this by a chain connected to my ankle.

Centurion farty breath bent down until his face was in mine, I held my breath, "Do you know who I am boy," he bellowed,

I felt like telling him that I wasn't deaf and there was toothpaste in my suitcase which he would be more than welcome to,

"No I don't," I said quickly trying not to breathe through my nose

"NO I DON'T, SIR!"

he roared even louder. "My name is Maximus Nasticus and I'm the meanest son of a Roman soldier you'll ever meet, I'm so mean they can't even stand me back in Rome and that's why I'm stuck here in your God forsaken country, do you understand,"

"Yes,"

"YES SIR!!!!!" he bellowed back at me with breath that I'm sure would strip the paint from our Moggie.

"Yes Sir," I said meekly, my eyes stinging from the pungent aroma.

"Don't even think about escape boy, if I catch you tampering with these shackles, I'll eat your liver for breakfast!"

And for a moment I wondered if that was why his breath smelt so bad.

"Tomorrow we'll take you into the fort for interrogation, that's if you survive the night, what is that thing you sit on boy,"

"Its my suitcase Sir,"

he didn't ask, he just pulled it from underneath me, flipping me over so that I went head first into the snow.

By the time I'd got up and brushed the snow from my eyes I saw him disappear into the tent opposite, it was getting dark, the fire was low and my teeth began to chatter.

All the Romans were now safely tucked up in their beds and I could hear a whole choir of snoring, except Nasticus, his silhouette was visible from the light in his tent, he had his great jewelled sword in his hand, bringing it down time after time on what I presumed was my suitcase.

I could hear him cursing in his own language, and it cheered me up no end, I knew there was no way he could get into the suitcase.

After a while the flap of his tent opened and the suitcase came flying out, landing only a few feet from me, he stuck his head out into the night air his breath visible in the cold and screamed something in frustration.

I would never know what words came out, but roughly translated I would hazard a guess that it was "Stupid suitcase!"

I smiled as he shut the flap behind him.

The chain around my ankle was short and as hard as I stretched the suitcase remained just out of reach, I just couldn't make it. There was no more light, no moon no stars, the sky covered in thick dark cloud, it was freezing and only a feeble orange glow came from the fire, any warmth had long since gone.

Just then I felt a rough hand on my shoulder, it was one of the Roman soldiers, he held his index finger up to his mouth telling me not to make a noise.

Then slowly he reached under his long red cape, my heart missed a beat, but instead of the dagger I expected, he produced a bundle of firewood,

"Thank you," I chattered through my vibrating molars.

"Listen carefully, just put one piece on at a time, otherwise Nasticus will be on to you, there's just enough to get you to morning,"

I thanked him again, he winked just like Dad did and disappeared. The burning wood gave off just enough heat so that I didn't freeze solid, I was really grateful to the soldier and in the morning he was pleased to see me still alive and smiled.

On the other hand Nasticus looked quite upset that he was still stuck with a small pyjama'd Briton, he picked up the suitcase and threw it in my direction, "Carry it boy," and then to everyone else "Break camp!"

Big flakes of snow began to fall as we set off, occasionally I spotted some people in the distance, but they soon made themselves scarce, when they saw Nasticus and his men marching towards them.

One of my slippers fell off in the deep snow, as I stopped to try and pick it up the soldier behind me pushed me hard, so hard that I was sent sprawling and slid for several feet on my freezing cold belly.

"Keep marching Briton, or Nasticus will have you for his breakfast, he likes small children, but rarely eats a full one," and he laughed at his own joke.

Nevertheless my little forced slide had given me an idea, I just had to wait for the right moment.

15. No More Telly

We'd been marching for about ten miles, it had stopped snowing and periodically clear patches of blue peaked through the white cloud.

To our left was a small hillock where a family of rabbits had crept out to nibble on the fresh green shoots, that had popped up through the melting snow. I estimated it must be spring time, still marching and without turning I decided to ask the question I'd been burning to ask since I arrived,

"Excuse me sir, but could you tell me the date?"

"March!" he shouted, prodding me again,

I was sick of this and angrily replied

"I am marching!"

"No you stupid Briton, it's March, no wonder you lot never beat us, you don't even know what month it is, I don't know why we're even bothering to colonise this place, you're all thick as ox dung!"

"Yer know, the only thing you Britons are good at, is getting drunk and fighting, thing is you don't know how to work as a team."

"Last February we had this massive battle with some of your lot up north, we were out-numbered three to one and still beat you easily, no battle plan yer see, the old Druids just wind you up into a frenzy then you came charging at us."

"Very brave, but very stupid, your warriors don't even wear armour, of all the places in all the world your people are the thickest I've ever come across and the Druids well.....if there was a place called 'Stupid Land' they would be it's rulers."

I couldn't shut him up once he'd got started, "Now Greece, there's a nice place, lovely food, nice climate, beautiful women, wine......... and the people, cracking people, academics, intelligent yer know, not like your Druids, your not a Druid are you boy?"

"No, I'm a school kid," I said.......I hesitated......."so what year is it?"

"It's AD44, do you know, I do believe you're even thicker than a Druid!"

AD44! AD44! it just kept going round and round in my head, I wouldn't be born for hundreds and hundreds of years, even my Grandad wouldn't be born for hundreds and hundreds of years!

How on earth can I get back to my own time, I can't live without television, fizzy pop and football, the key must be the suitcase. When I jumped into it, or should I say when Lenny made me jump into it (I'll kill him when I get back!) I somehow travelled through space and time, to end up here in AD44, Roman occupied Britain.

The first chance I get, I must jump back into the case and hopefully end up back in my room, with the Beast from Mars and the Beast from across our street, Lenny! I decided that when I do get back, I would take a snow ball and stuff it down Lenny's pyjamas.

The soldier behind me was still twittering on about how even Gaul was better than this (something) place, he swore really badly and I really shouldn't repeat it!

"There it is Druid boy your new home, lovely isn't it."

It wasn't lovely, it was horrible, we had climbed to the top of a steep hill and below us was a snow filled valley.

Meandering through the middle of the valley was a wide river and along it's bank, what looked like lots of little huts, a village I supposed. But towering above all of this was a great wooden fort, with sentries marching around the tops of the walls, just to it's left was another huge building still under construction, it was covered in a maze of wooden scaffolding.

I could see small figures working all along the scaffolding, like little ants busying themselves with the giant task in hand. "Lovely, innit," said the chatty Roman,

"That's the new fort, that is, and you see them woods behind, well we've marched all this way to chop em down, for the timber to build the new fort, bit more impressive than your wooden huts eh, thicko!"

"Sting won't like it," I said, he didn't answer. "Well Rabitticus, why have we stopped, having a little chin wag are we, you 'orrible little legionairre!" Nasticus bellowed down the chatty Roman's earhole,

"Sorry sir, don't know sir, c'mon Druid boy move," and he clipped me around the side of the head as if it was my fault he'd stopped.

We were moving down the other side of the hill, it was hard to keep my balance, my feet were so cold I could barely feel them and I still had only one slipper, Mum would kill me for that.

If they ever got me in that fort and took my suitcase, I was stuck here for life, it was now or never.

Fortunately I was being marched at the front of the column, I started to slow down on purpose, and as expected Rabitticus started to nudge and push me impatiently.

"RABITTICUS!" screamed Nasticus from somewhere behind us, "Move it you fat lard-like dumpling or I'll make a pin cushion out of your backside!"

Rabitticus was scared now, and he took it out on me! He raised his leg, placed his foot in the small of my back and pushed with all his fear. I soared through the air, but I was expecting it, I was prepared.

In mid flight I placed the suitcase under my chest and landed as smooth as vanilla milk shake, I lifted my legs slightly and I was away, tobogganing down the hillside at tremendous speed and for the first time in ancient history the world heard the name "Geronimooooooo!"

The suitcase was zipping across the snow flakes, spray flying up at the sides and in my face, in the distance I could hear Nasticus yelling and telling his men to take out their bows, BOWS!

Swish an arrow flew past my right ear and stuck in the ground in front of me, it snapped with a thwacking noise as the suitcase slid over it, other arrows fell, but none came quite that close and soon I was out of range.

As I looked over my shoulder, I could see Nasticus still yelling at the top of the hill, while his men were charging after me swords drawn, but falling comically in the snow.

I'd made it, whuuuumpf! I knew I shouldn't have thought that, for no sooner than I had, I hit a huge rocky outcrop which acted as a ramp and I was now flying through the air turning full circle.

Splat, I landed again, fortunately the right way up and I carried on careering down the slope faster than ever, the huts, the river, the people and the fort were all very rapidly becoming larger and larger as I drew near.

The fort was not going to be a problem, I was well to the right hand side of it, the village and the river would be!

One or two of the villager's spotted this strange sight heading towards them, a boy from the 20th Century skimming through the snow at great speed on a brown leather suitcase, wearing blue and white striped pyjamas and one slipper, and they looked suitably shocked.

Legs disappeared to my left and my right, as they tried to get out of my way, one set of legs stayed.

At the far end of the village stood a great hairy Roman soldier holding his sword with both hands high above his head, his gaze firmly fixed on me. I was heading straight towards him and there was nothing I could do, I put my hands over my head, closed my eyes and hoped he'd miss.

He did, and I flew right between his legs, "Nutmeg," I shouted as I whizzed underneath him, this is a football term used when you put the ball between someone's legs, I don't know why I said it, I think it was some kind of nervous reaction.

I was quickly leaving the village behind me, in front the land seemed to simply disappear, it was the bank of the river.

I was flying through the air again, this time heading for a severe soaking, but no it didn't happen, now I knew what it felt like to be one of the stones I skimmed on the big pond at the sand hills.

The suitcase, with me on it, skimmed five great leaps across the river and flew between two large trees on the opposite bank, there was little snow on the ground now, I was entering the woods and consequently I gradually began to slow down.

I managed to narrowly avoid a couple of painful looking trees, but ahead was one I surely wouldn't miss, I crossed all my fingers and hoped I would slow to a halt.

Slowing, slowing, slowing but still too fast, there was something at the base of the tree, I couldn't make it out,

"Oh my!" it couldn't be, it was!

At the base of the tree was the strangest sight I had ever seen, lying down on it's back, was a bull, with enormous horns, but strangest of all was the fact that it had it's arms behind the back of it's head, in a human-like relaxed position.

I couldn't move, I was scared, it was silly, I couldn't take my eyes off it, then, CRASH! I hit it smack on, I lay on the floor quite dazed, head spinning.

The last thing I remember was looking upwards as I lay on my back, tree tops spinning round like a green-brown kaleidascope, and then the beast's head coming towards me nostrils flaring and a great white beard..........a great white beard!?!

I passed out...........

16. A Druid called Duncan

I couldn't tell you how long I'd been out for, but when I did wake up, I was no longer under the tree. I was lying on a big furry animal skin on the floor of a large hut and on top of me were even more animal skins.

This was the warmest I had been for some time and if it wasn't for the fact that I was in a strange place in AD44, I would have been quite happy to stay in this hairy bed for a few more hours.

I got up on my elbows and looked around, it was a circular hut, with a thatched roof, a small fire burning in the middle of the room, there was no chimney so consequently the ceiling was covered in a thick layer of smoke.

Coming from somewhere was a terrible smell and I was quite sure it wasn't the fire, it could have been a nearby farm as it definitely smelt like pooh!

I propped myself up further and sniffed the air, it was then that I saw 'The Beast,' it was here, in the hut, on my bed, somehow it had crept up on me!

It's massive horned head was actually resting on my chest, inches away from my face, I pulled my legs up smartly and kicked it full force in what must have been it's belly and it flew into the air, quickly I rolled and as it came back down again I dived upon its back.

I'd been thumping it for over a minute when I realised it hadn't put up any resistance, I'd grabbed it's horns and twisted it's head this way and that and punched it on the nose repeatedly, with no response at all.

"I think you'll find that's totally unnecessary," said a soft voice from behind me, I spun round falling off my victim to see an extremely long white beard.

"Thank you for coming, I was expecting you, although I wasn't expecting you to arrive in quite the manner you did."

"You, you, you're the bulls beard," I finally blurted out.

"I am I suppose, the bull is only a skin of course as you can now see, so beating it about the head won't do you any good at all,"

"I don't understand, where am I, how did I get here and who are you?"

"Well to begin with you are in my hut at the southerly end of the Great Wood, I carried you here when you were knocked out colliding with myself and the tree, and finally I am Duncan the local Druid."

"I hope that answers all your questions, now how are those feet, you had quite a nasty case of frostbite when I brought you here."

I poked my feet out from beneath the furry duvet and to my horror both of my feet had turned completely black, and smelt like something rotting in the bottom of a compost heap! All this time I thought we were somewhere near a farm, and all this time it was my feet turning black and about ready to drop off.

The Druid must have seen the look of great concern on my face and gently laughed,

"Oh don't worry, that's not your feet that's my special remedy for frostbite, I didn't study to be a Druid for twenty years without learning basic frostbite treatment, never very good at seeing the future, but best in my year at bursting boils and frostbite,

I have a certificate for it somewhere."

"Come along over here and we'll make them as good as new,"

he motioned me towards the fire and a large black metal bowl resting beside it,

"Come sit here" he slid a wooden stool up along side the bowl.

"Now then," he said scratching his chin through his long white beard,

"How does it go, what words, what words?" "Oh aye, that's it, right place your feet in the bowl." I gently eased my feet into the warm water, it was a nice feeling and reminded me of the hot bath Dad had run for me, the night I returned with the suitcase.

71

The suitcase! "My suitcase, where's my suitcase, you didn't leave it in the woods did you, tell me you didn't leave it in the woods!"

For a moment the old feller looked confused, "Aha, the box, it's the box you're speaking of, tush no, it's just there and quite safe," and there it was by the side of my scary-hairy bed, my ticket home.

"Oh Ceaser's bottom, you've made me forget," he exclaimed in frustration,

"I'm sorry, forget what," I apologised,

"I don't know, I've forgotten,"

"I think you were looking for some words,"

"Of course I was, of course I was, silly me, now then are you sitting comfortably," I nodded and he began...............

> *"Rotting meat of smelly feet,*
> *Make thine skin and toes complete,*
> *Dung of cow and squirrels nose,*
> *Let this lad keep all his toes."*

He beckoned me with his long boney fingers to raise my feet out of the water and when I did they were glowing and pink.

He counted my toes, "eight!" he exclaimed triumphantly

"Only joking, us Druids like to have a bit of a joke you know, you did have ten to begin with didn't you?" I nodded.

"Told you, best in my year, I think you'll play football again after all, by the way what exactly is football?"

For the next half hour I explained all about the world's greatest game, he was very interested and kept making notes in a little book. When I finished I asked, "But how do you know about football and what you said earlier, you were expecting me, how can that be?"

"It's quite a long story, but I'll try to make it as brief as possible, I am the Druid for the two neighbouring villages, one you have already seen on the other side of the river, the poor people there live under strict Roman rule and fear of Nasty."

"You mean Nasticus,"

"Yes, but everyone calls him Nasty for short, I'm sure you understand,"

"Oh yeah," I knew only too well.

The other village is hidden deep in the forest, as yet the Romans do not know of it's existence, I say as yet because tomorrow they start to chop down the Great Wood, many people, many animals and many plants will lose their home and many may even lose their lives."

"I was once respected by both village's, and now they have sought my help to deal with the Romans, but I do not have the power."

"I am trained to heal, to advise people on when to plant crops, to tell them the future, to pass on wisdom and to see that they follow the laws of the land, I am not a warrior or a wizard, I am just an educated man, what can I do against the might of the Roman army?"

"That still doesn't answer my question,"

"If you'll just let me finish, I did say it was a long story, did I not?"

"Sorry," I apologised,

"Well I was at my wit's end, by now nobody in either village would have anything to do with me, I was kicked out and now live here alone, worthless and jobless, do you know what that's like?"

I don't know why, but I thought of Dad and my eyes filled with tears,

"I see that you do," said the Druid tenderly and this time he apologised.

"I studied my books, to try and find something to use against the Romans, but there was nothing. I needed help, so in desperation I decided to evoke the spirit of the Green Man."

"The Green Man!"

I wondered if he was the bloke on the tin of sweet corn, "So who is this Green Man?" The old man looked to the skies and went on.

"The Green Man is a mighty spirit, the spirit of nature, the spirit of life, protector of the Great Wood only he could advise me."

"To do this I had to first skin a bull, a very messy job I might add, then wrapped in the bull's skin lie on a bed of rowan branches, beneath a great oak, fall asleep and dream."

"And I dreamt, like I have never dreamt before." "The Green Man came to me and he said

'Do not fear oh faithful Druid, all is not lost, when things seem at there darkest, a ray of light will shine and all will be well, so be it," and he was gone.

"And then images, the like I have never seen, I saw you, I saw you battling the striped beast to gain the box over yonder, I saw Leonard the Liar and Dougie the Squire, I'm sorry I do tend to talk in rhyme sometimes, it's a Druid thing."

"It's okay, please go on," I said.

"I saw great metal beasts of burden with wheels, I saw a box with pictures and sound, I saw fizzy pop, I saw a single tooth surrounded by foam and I saw football, but most of all I saw you."

"I knew you were the one, I knew you were coming, I knew you had the power to help us against our enemies for the Green Man foretold it, and then I awoke and you were there."

I didn't know what to say, how could I help these people, I had no power, I felt sorry for the Druid and grateful for the kindness he'd shown me but I was just a kid, what could I do!

I made my mind up, all I had to do was humour the old boy for a while, wait until he's safely out of the way, jump back into the suitcase and get back to my video, sleep-over, home and normal things.

I felt guilty for even having such thoughts, the old man was looking at me "Are you well, young sir?"

"Yes, I'm fine, just thinking," I replied, I felt even worse now, I was his one hope and I was about to dessert.

I decided I must at the very least thank him for looking after me "..........and sorry," I said "What's your name I didn't catch it in all the confusion"?

"My name is Duncan the Druid, young sir, and I too must apologise for I have not asked after your identity,"

"Oh me, my name's Raymond Thursday, but you can call me Ray, only my Mum calls me Raymond."

Duncan the Druid's eyes glazed over as if in a trance and he spoke in an eerie voice

"A Ray of light will shine and all will be well." he smiled "You ARE the one!"

17. The List Complete!

His shiny white beard almost reached his knees and his hair went half way down his back, if he was back in my time he could possibly be an ageing member of a once great rock band.

Most of that day we talked, he said it would not be safe for me to go out in daylight, as Nasticus would have his men out looking for me.

We had a kind of porridge for breakfast, with honey to sweeten it and it wasn't half bad, for lunch we had porridge, then at dinner we had porridge, I was getting sick of it already.

Duncan said that there was plenty left for supper if I was peckish, for all the sorrow the Romans were causing the ancient Britons I felt they had to be congratulated for inventing the pizza.

Late in the evening Duncan slipped on a long black hooded robe, "I must go out for a short while, please make yourself at home,"

I crossed my fingers and hoped he wasn't about to offer me more porridge, thankfully he never. He only got half way to the door

"There's something I wanted to say, emm I'm er going to collect mistletoe, midnight's always best, so you just em, you know, feel free to um.......and I'll be back shortly."

This time he made it all the way to the door and stopped,

"So you'll be alright while I'm gone?"

"I'll be fine," I said,

"Good, fine, right..........anything I can get you, no of course not, oh dog's droppings, I'm so sorry but I just have to ask."

"That's alright ask anything you like," I said smiling at his awkwardness,

"Well oh Ray of Light, what exactly are you going to do to those horrible Romans?"

"Please don't call me that, it's just Ray okay," "Of course I'm sorry, Ray okay what will you do to them," and he rubbed his hands together in glee.

"Good question, to tell you the truth I haven't got a clue, after all I'm only a little kid."

He was totally happy with this answer, "Don't you worry Ray you'll think of something by morning, I know you will," he slammed the door merrily behind and was gone.

It wasn't fair, what could I do, I wasn't Frederick Challenger, he would have probably taken his double barrel shotgun to them and frightened them off once and for all.

It was hopeless, I was useless and poor Duncan had so much faith in me, I had to leave before I made Duncan look even more worthless in front of his people.

I found his notebook and scribbled, 'Dear Duncan, I am so sorry I cannot help you, I am just a young frightened boy not the ray of light you were told of, I really wish I could help, please apologise to the Green Man for me, thank you for your kindness, and signed it Raymond Thursday.

I threw the suitcase on the floor "Yad Sruht Dnom Yar," a clicking, a whirring and it was open, I took one last look around the Druids hut and jumped.

My feet landed firmly on something so I opened my eyes, I was still in the hut, I quickly tried again only to find I was going nowhere!

Why wouldn't it work, was I stuck here forever, no that couldn't be it, in my mind I saw Mr. Buckingham that night on the beach and remembered the last thing he said to me.

"Remember Raymond with the suitcase comes great responsibility," this is what he must have been talking about, I was here to help and until I did, I could not return!

I stepped out of the suitcase feeling slightly ashamed, I had to think, for tomorrow I had to face Nasticus and his men,

"Well I'm certainly not going to do it, wearing my pyjamas that's for sure,"
I said out loud and began to unpack the clothes from my case.

Within moments I was dressed, once more looking like a mini Frederick Challenger, everything fit perfectly and I somehow felt better about my prospects with the Romans.

"Ow!" something was sticking in my shoulder blades, I wriggled around trying to feel what it was, "Well done Ray," I said to myself.

I'd only put my shirt on with the coat hanger still inside it. Reaching down inside my collar I managed to grab it and tried to manoeuvre it out the back of my shirt, it slipped several times and then I got it by the hook, I undid the top two shirt buttons with free hand, so that I could pull it out.

I was sweating now, this was hard work, but I was determined to at least win my battle with the coat hanger.

Wrapping my hand around the hook I gave it a good tug, "Ouch!" my head crashed against something hard and I was completely engulfed in smoke.

My eyes were streaming from the stinging smoke, I couldn't understand what was happening, the only explanation was that the hut had caught fire, I ran in the direction of the doorway.

My feet were going as fast as I could make them, but I wasn't getting anywhere, it was like one of those horrible dreams when something terrible is coming after you, and it's as if your feet are stuck in thick mud.

I looked down at my brown boots to see them running at full speed, no mud, no nothing, absolutely nothing!

I gulped when I realised there was no floor beneath my revolving feet, through the smoke I could just make out beneath me the round circular room, the small fire still burning, the animal skins where I'd slept and my pyjamas, strewn across the floor where I'd dropped them in my haste to get changed.

It was hard to breathe up here in the smoke let alone think, maybe all that porridge had filled me with so much gas I was now lighter than air, I tried burping a few times but nothing happened, my head was softly bouncing off the spiky ceiling, it hurt.

With both hands I pushed myself away from it, but as soon as I did, I plummeted like a rock towards the hard clay floor, I was screaming, in a couple of seconds I would be a nasty mess on Duncan's floor.

The coat hanger, that was it! 'The coat hanger FLIES, not goes, as I'd put in the direction you pull,' I quickly reached down the back of my collar, oh no it had slipped down again, got it! I held the hook of the hanger in my right hand, still screaming, the floor racing to meet me and pulled with all my might, whooosh, thwack, crunch!

Mere inches before hitting solid ground I had once again defied gravity, I had also overdone it slightly. I'd pulled on the hanger so hard that I had not only gone back up, but I'd gone right through the ceiling and was now soaring up into the cold night sky, I could see the hut beneath me on the edge of the woods, getting smaller and smaller, as I steadily climbed.

I realised I was still pulling and still screaming so immediately shut my mouth, and as soon as I stopped pulling the hook of the hanger my flight into the starry sky slowed, until I was hovering gently in pretty much the same position.

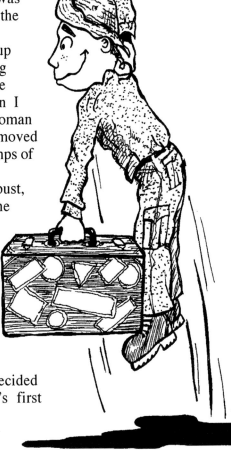

It was an amazing sight from up here the Moon lit up the meandering river like a shiny snail trail, the Great Wood was even larger than I imagined and I could see both Roman forts, little lights like glow worms moved around the battlements from the lamps of the Roman sentries.

My heart was still beating fit to bust, I wanted my feet firmly on the ground and so pushed the coat hanger downwards, gently this time, and floated slowly back down through the small hole I'd made in the roof.

As I landed safely on the floor of the hut, I looked upwards at the stars through the gap in the thatch, there was no more smoke and I proudly decided that I had just invented Britain's first chimney.

Now to experiment with my new found power of flight,

I placed a single finger under the hook and with the slightest of pressure pulled.

My feet rose several inches above the ground, I stopped pulling and hovered, a slight tug to the left and I moved left, right and I moved to the right.

It was easy and before long I was doing huge circular laps of the room, I finally came in to land, excited and elated perhaps now I really could help Duncan and the villagers.

The only way to stop flying around was to release the pressure from the hook of the hanger and as I did so, I gently floated back to earth. I took it out and examined it more closely than I had before, on the wooden part there was some writing, I smiled as I read it 'Steller Airlines' and underneath, 'We hope you enjoyed your flight.'

Placing it back in the suitcase I began to realise why Freddy had put so much importance on the case, it truly was wonderful.

All this excitement had given me an appetite and believe it or not I finished off the porridge, I could still smell a farm nearby but had definitely not spotted one when flying above the surrounding area.

At last I realised the farm smell was me, I hadn't washed or cleaned my teeth in two days, Mum would kill me if she were here.

On the table was a large bowl and a jug, so I set about cleaning myself up, there were no mirrors but by the speed the clear water turned black I judged I must have been pretty mucky, I must admit I never actually thought that the soap and the toothpaste would ever be any use.

I was just buttoning up my shirt when Duncan came through the door, with a bunch of mistletoe under his arm, "I'm back," he called "Good night for mistletoe I see," I responded cheerfully.

He stopped dead in his tracks, turned a very peculiar colour, and then straight as a plank fell backwards. Hastily I dashed over to his fallen body, he was still breathing, he must have passed out, why I had no idea.

I took the flask off my belt and sprinkled some water over his face, he moaned a little and gradually opened his eyes.

"Duncan, it's me Ray are you alright, can you hear me?" he just stared at me, "Hello Duncan, it's me are you receiving me, over!" I always said stupid things at the most stressful times.

"Ray, oh Ray is that really you, did the Romans find you, did it hurt, where have they put your head," he was babbling, making no sense.

I poured the entire contents of my canteen over his wrinkled hairy face,

"Come on Duncan, snap out of it, your talking gibberish,"

"Will you please stop that, I am quite awake, thank you"
there was a definite hint of annoyance in his voice.

"Okay, I'm sorry," I said
"But you were saying such strange things," standing he beckoned me to follow him to the large metal bow.

"Look," he said a softness now returning to his voice, we both peered over the rim of the bowl at the same time.

It was incredibly strange and extremely spooky, there was Duncan's reflection as clear as day, droplets of water still running down his beard, and me, well there was a shirt!

I stepped back in horror, I could feel my face, my hair, they were still there and my hands, I was obviously using them, they were in front of my face yet I could see right through them.

I had at last found the one missing word from Frederick Challenger's list, 'Something' soap only works for thirty minutes............and that 'something' was 'Invisible'!

18. The Flying Shrub

And true enough it proved to be, within a short time I gradually started to become visible again, just to make sure and to test the soap, I washed my feet complete with boots and socks in the large metal bowl.

It was weird watching them quickly fade away and approximately thirty minutes later re-appear, I could have great fun with this at school, if I ever get back.

Turning to the old Druid I asked "Tell me something Duncan, when you saw the Green Man what did he look like?"

"Oh he was a magnificent sight, long flowing hair and a mighty beard, a crown of leaves upon his head and of course completely green from head to toe."

"He was kind and gentle when he spoke to me, but just like nature he can be hard, cruel and extremely powerful!"

"My Dad once told me, that the force of nature is the most powerful thing on this planet,"

"Your Father is indeed a wise man and has taught you well, but now as the tribes of Britain are broken up and fragmented by the Roman legions, we no longer seem to have the unity of mind to call upon our great spirits."

"Perhaps it is time to give the people back that faith, perhaps it's time for the Green Man to return!" I said defiantly,
a plan was hatching somewhere deep in my brain.
"Do the Romans know of the Green Man?"

"Yes they know the stories and laugh at them, they have beaten us so many times in battle, they have taxed and broken the will of the people, then they ask where is your Green Man?"

"Hiding in the woods? perhaps he should be called the Yellow Man, and then they hop around like chickens, it's so embarrassing especially to us Druids."

"The people of our country see this, then they too begin to disbelieve and so without belief the power of the Green Man fades, until soon he will be no more than a story parents tell their children at bed time."

"Duncan, tomorrow the Green Man will return to these woods and the Romans will run away like frightened children!"

"Go to both villages tonight, right now in fact, tell them this and tell them to meet here at first light........oh and by the way, can you get hold of any paint or dye from the village?"

He already had his black hooded robe on and was about to leave "Yes," he said a curious look flashing across his wrinkly forehead.

"Great, make sure you bring some back with you," and he was gone.
A moment later he made me jump, when he stuck his great white head through the open window "What colour?"

"Green of course!"
he smiled and disappeared into the night.

Now it was my turn, I had much to do before morning.
I took the coat hanger out of my suitcase and eased it under the back of my collar, hooking it on so that it would not slip down, with some heavy string from the hut I strapped my suitcase to my chest, and cautiously stepped outside into the darkness of the Great Wood.

Down by the river bank I collected huge leaves and ferns, arranging them all over myself until I looked like a camouflaged soldier, who'd gone slightly over the top, a little fat shrub wearing brown boots.

I reached back, found the hook of the hanger and soared into the air, heading towards the Roman fort, the only sound was the breeze rustling through my leaves and the distant chatter of Roman sentries.

I pulled back on the coat hanger and hovered some fifty feet above the fort and soldiers below, my heart was beating fast as I began my slow descent, still unsure of exactly what I was about to do.

"What butties have you got tonight Phillipus?"

"Wild Boar and cress, what about you?"

"Yak's cheese, again, don't suppose you want to swap?"

"For yak's cheese! no thanks mate, gives me terrible wind that stuff, I'll be blasting off all night and the lad's in the barracks will kick me out into the freezing cold corridor!"

"Yeah, but just think, you could probably blast those stupid woods down in one great fart, and save us all that work tomorrow."

They both laughed,

"Flippin' cold sitting up here innit, I don't know why they insist we wear these little red skirts, not exactly the climate for it."

"Four pair of underpants, that's what you need otherwise you'll get piles, my old Mum told me that." I hovered above them for a while until eventually I had an idea.

Silently I floated down until I was directly behind them, they were sat quite close together, the space in between them taken up by their half eaten sandwiches.

At precisely the same moment, I stretched out my arms and tapped them both on their opposite shoulders. Immediately they turned to look in that direction, at which time I deftly swapped their sandwiches around and hovered above them again.

"Oooooh spooky this place innit?"

"Was that you" "Was that me, what?"

"Tapping me on my shoulder?"

"No, honest, somebody tapped mine too,"

"You're right it is a spooky place," and they both picked up their sandwiches together. "Phlaargh!" the Roman with the unexpected mouthful of yak's cheese spat it out on the others red skirt,

"Now look what you've done," he yelled standing quickly and scraping the yellow semi-digested goo from the red material.

"ME, ME! it's you, you crafty sheep turd, you swapped butties when I wasn't looking!"

"Don't you call me a sheep turd, Nasticus Breath!"

"Oh that's really pushing it now, anymore of that and I'll punch your flippin' lights out!"

Yeah, you and whose army, shorty,"

"Shuddup!" "You shuddup!" "No you shuddup!"

"I said it first!" "Didn't!" "Did!"

"Or, just put a Briton's sock in it!"

At this point they both swung around on the bench so that they now had their backs to each other, arms folded like sullen children.

I silently descended once more, flicked the big one on his ear as hard as I could, and popped back up to a safe distance.

"Right that's it pal, you're dead meat!" The smaller one looked shocked and tried to plead his innocence, but was abruptly stopped in mid sentence by a huge fist in his face! I held my hand over my mouth to stop giggling as the Roman was sent sprawling across the floor.

The smaller one got to his feet holding his nose "What was that for?" he said as if speaking through his nose,

"Shuddup, I'm not talking to you anymore!" They both returned to their seats, I descended and flicked the big guy's ear even harder than before, and all hell broke loose.

Before long the clamour and commotion caused by the two scrapping soldiers had attracted the attention of all the other sentries on duty. They tried to break it up, but ended up joining in and before long there must have been fifty of them knocking ten bells out of each other.

Now to get their attention,

"Roman Legionairres" I screamed in a high pitched spooky type of voice, they stopped and looked around in bewilderment.

I floated down to their level, I kept my distance though and when I glanced down I could see the river below me, I must have been a good eight feet from the fort's wall.

"Roman Legionairres"

I shrieked once more and they immediately gathered at the edge of the battlements, jostling for the best view.

"Who said that, who's out there!"

"It is I, Shrub Man messenger of the great spirit of the woods!"

They all 'oooooooeeed' together, the same sort of 'ooooooooh' the audience does on a T.V. quiz show, when they show you the star prize.

"Do not fight amongst yourselves Romans, for tomorrow you must face the might of the Green Man!"

Some of them started to laugh at this,

"Oooooh! the Green Man, we're really scared of him aren't we lads!"

"Fly away little bush, before we put you in a pot with some donkey manure!" They laughed even more, this wasn't exactly going to plan, I pulled the hook as hard as I could and flew straight at them, knocking four or five of them over, quickly returning to my hovering position and cackled like a witch.

"You won't be laughing tomorrow!"

They all 'Ooooooeed' again, I could hear some of them at the back talking,

"My Mum had a bush just like that one." "Look it's wearing little brown boots!"

"Silence!" I shrieked, I'm sure I'm going to have a sore throat in the morning.

"Out of the way lads, I'll sort this little weed out," the big Roman who'd started the fight was pushing his way to the front. In his hand he held a spear which he threw at me with all his might, he was too close, there was no time to move, it flew straight and true, it penetrated my leafy disguise and hit the suitcase with a loud thud.

I was glad it made a loud thud, as the noise covered the sound of all the breath leaving my body.

The spear fell hundreds of feet to the river below, meanwhile Shrub Man was winded, the Romans were 'Oooooing' again and the big Roman had just passed out.

At least I'd finally got their attention.

I moved closer to them, this time they backed off "Tomorrow" I cackled "The Green Man will have Roman soldiers for breakfast!"

I cackled like the craziest witch you could ever imagine, and the soldiers as a unit turned and ran screaming back down the steps and into the relative safety of the fort.

I'd done it, I'd put the wind up them good and proper.

As I flew back over the woods towards Duncan's hut I allowed myself a victory smile, but only for a brief moment.

For tomorrow with Nasticus to lead them, it wouldn't be quite as easy.

19. A Good Day to Die

Duncan was nudging me in the ribs, "Come on Master Raymond, you really must wake up."

"Just five more minutes Mum."

"Raymond please, the sun is rising and the day of reckoning is upon us."

In that fleeting moment when you're neither asleep or awake, I thought I was back home and it was time for school, it was quite a shock when I opened my eyes and I was still in the great hut.

Duncan's smiling face greeted me,

"Hello there, glad you could join us back in the land of the living."

"Eh! oh yeah, morning Duncan, what time is it?"

"Time you were up young man, we have Romans to attend to."

I rolled back over in my bed and pulled the furry duvet over my head. "Do we have to, can't I just stay in bed and read the Beano?"

"You speakest in riddles Raymond, hurry now or your porridge will be cold." "Oh great more Porridge!"

"I sense from your tone you do not like my porridge." I felt guilty now "No I love it Duncan, honest."

And with that I dragged myself from my bed and sat at the wooden table, to face another huge bowl of steaming porridge,

"Mmmmmm yummy," I purred slopping great spoonfuls of the grey mixture into my mouth, the Druid looked at me, one eyebrow raised, as if to say don't over do it.

I couldn't help but smile at him,

"How come you've never had kids Duncan?"

"I did have some once, but they ate my tunic and a large portion of my roof, terrible animals."

"No I mean children!" "Oh them, no never, oooh horrid things! I think I would prefer to have the baby goats eating my home, than noisy children running around everywhere."

I could just see Duncan's children being sent off to school with a lunch box full of dripping porridge sandwiches.

"Something amusing you?" he enquired,

I must have been smiling at the thought of it all,

"No I was just thinking of you as a Dad, you'd be good at it," he muttered something under his breath, whilst clearing the bowls away.

The Druid quickly returned with two large mugs of water, and sat opposite me a look of anticipation in his eyes.

"Okay, I've come up with a plan" I said,

"It's probably completely stupid, but well, this is it,"

for the next half hour or so I poured out the idea I'd had the previous night and told him of Shrub Man's little adventure.

When I finished he just stared at me, my plan was obviously not very good.

Then suddenly and without warning he leapt into the air clapping his hands above his head, which then led into a little Druid jig around the table.

Grabbing my hands he made me dance around the table too,

"Raymond my wonderful boy, you're a veritable genius!"

Then just as suddenly he stopped,

"Oh dear, Oh dear, oh dear, we'll never get them to do it, they're so stubborn," and he slumped back into his chair,

"What, who," I squeaked.

"The warriors, they have such strong traditions in battle, I really don't know if they'll agree to this?"

"I'm sure we can persuade them, just this once Dunc, we can tell them that I am a messenger from the Green Man, and this is what he wants them to do."

"But surely Raymond that would involve telling an untruth, I would be breaking my solemn vow as a Druid, if it ever got out no one would ever trust me again!"

"Duncan, I'm really sorry to say this, but nobody trusts you now, that's why you're here living alone on the edge of the woods."

The Druids shoulders sunk as I spoke,
"Don't you see, this way we can win back their faith, we can unite the village's against the Romans, save the woods and save your job at the same time."

"His head rose slowly at first "By Ceaser's knickers you're right, I can manage one little white lie, if it's for the good of the people."

The more I got to know him the more I liked him, he never gave a single thought for himself, only his people.

Just then came a tremendous pounding on the wooden door, so tremendous that the very hut shook, small pieces of branches from the thatched roof began falling like snowflakes all around us.

"Aha that will be 'The Ram', punctual as ever," "The Ram'! I gulped as he swung open the door to reveal the largest human being I have ever seen in my life!

"Come in my son, come in, it's good to see you again"
the huge being crouched as he came through the door, his shoulder so wide he could barely squeeze them through the frame.

He must have been eight foot tall, arms like tree trunks, head shaved and if he did have a neck on those mighty shoulders it was completely covered by a fiery red beard.

"Ram, my boy, this is Raymond, he has come very far to help us."
the very ground shook as he lumbered towards me, my hand disappeared inside his, as he shook it, much gentler than I would have imagined.

"Welcome Ray Man, this is a good day to die, yes!" he said far too cheerfully.
I pulled my hand away quickly
"No!" I gulped
"Definitely not, but today is a good day for chasing Romans out of this part of Briton forever."

he roared a hearty laugh and replied
"That sounds like fun Ray Man, when can we start?"
Duncan slapped him on the back
"That's the spirit Ram, bring the rest of them inside will you?"
"Yes oh mighty Druid."
"Bless his baldy head." said Duncan his eyes misting over slightly,

"He's one of the few who's always had faith in me."

As the rest of the villagers filed into the hut I grabbed him by the wrist and whispered to him, "They all will after today."

Duncan took all the warriors to one side of the great hut, while on the other side the women, children and myself sat together crossed legged in a circle, myself in the middle.

They had never been involved in any kind of battle before, the warriors would not allow it, so they were all extremely excited and listened to the plan with wide eyes and looks of wonder.

Across the other side of the room, I could hear the disgruntled rumblings of the Celtic warriors, Duncan was struggling to make them see it his way.

"No, it's not my way either" I heard him shout "But it is the way of the Green Man!"

"This young man you see here," he said pointing his long finger at me "Has travelled through the centuries, from a Briton of the future, a Briton where no Roman invaders walk our land, a Briton that is free!"

"Do you want that freedom?" "Aye," they cheered as one,

"Then follow Raymond!" There was silence for what seemed like an eternity.

One voice at first, then two, a few more joined in and before long every person in the hut, from the smallest child to the meanest Celtic warrior was chanting

"Ray Man, Ray Man, Ray Man!"

Duncan came to me through the crowd, a smile as broad as the length of his beard and lifted me onto the table, I stood bewildered, embarrassed but smiling and gradually they fell silent.

The Ram stood up, he looked at me and then he looked at everyone in the room "I am not a wise man like our great Druid, I am a warrior, but I know men's hearts, I see the honesty in this boy and I pledge my sword to him," then smiling he turned to me

"Speak Ray Man." I gulped hard and spoke as clearly as I could,

"Thank you, everyone."

I was shaking and hoped they couldn't see,

"I don't know what to say, except you each know your jobs, good luck, let's go kick some Roman skirts!!"

The cheer nearly lifted the roof off.

20. Nice Undies!

When the cheer eventually died down, everyone of the villagers shook hands, hugged and wished each other luck, it was like going out for a cup final at Wembley Stadium. Within a few minutes the great hut was empty, only Duncan and I remained. "Okay Dunc, you know what to do."

"Yes everything is in readiness, and you?"

"I'm going on a little scouting trip to see how Nasty and his men are this morning." "Good luck oh mighty Druid," I said with a smile,

he smiled back "Good luck Ray Man," we shook hands and I was gone.

I walked through the woods, suitcase in hand feeling quite nervous about the coming events. I swung the suitcase up and caught it with both hands, and holding it straight out in front of me said "See the trouble, you've gotten me into!"

In the dense woods I could hear the river, long before I could see it, but now it opened out in front of me, rushing freezing cold water and I definitely preferred a bath nice and hot. I placed the suitcase down carefully on the grassy bank, the last thing I needed was for it to slip in the water and be carried off in the current.

The bank of the river was slippy, so I went down on my bottom, to my left the valley, the river, rolling hills, the morning mist still lingering and to my right the Celtic village overshadowed by the two forts. The thought of the Romans making the poor villagers lives a misery, gave me the courage to do what I had to do.

"Come on Ray, on three, THREE!"

Kerrsplosh! If you haven't slept for a few days and you've had a particularly stressful time, I strongly recommend you jump in a freezing cold river at first light, in the middle of winter.

For a few seconds the cold took my breath away completely and then it all came back at once "BRRRRRRRRRAAAGH!"

I shook myself life like a big wet dog and scrambled back out at a hundred miles an hour! From the suitcase I took a piece of the soap, considerably smaller now as I'd had to cut it up into little pieces, and began to give myself an all over wash, it was then that I noticed a large body of men and wagons leaving the fort.

They were heading over the bridge and towards the great woods, it was too early! I had to delay them somehow, or we wouldn't be ready and all our plans would be in vain.

Looking down I just had time to see my brown boots disappear, a quick wash for the coat hanger and suitcase and I was ready.

I pulled the hook and Whoooosh! zooming only four or five inches above the water I hurtled down river towards the bridge, and at the last moment banked to the left and hovered some distance in front of the soldiers, just above the tree tops at the entrance to the woods.

Many of the soldiers I had seen at the fort last night were in the work party, quite a few had black eyes from their fight and all of them looked very edgy. They were looking this way and that, no longer marching with their usual swagger, but timid little steps, Shrub Man had done a good job.

At the front of the two columns was the man himself, Maximus Nasticus, it may have been my imagination but I was sure I could smell his breath way up here, unfortunately he didn't look scared at all.

This had to be fast, I had to gain height so that I could gather enough speed. I flew straight up turned and plummeted towards the earth in front of the Romans, I had to time this just right, the ground was rushing to meet me at a frightening speed. At about Roman head height I pulled the hook into a horizontal position, now aiming right down the middle of the two columns of men.

Controlling the speed and flight with my right hand, I held the suit case in my left and clobbered every single Roman soldier in the left column across the forehead, fifty dented helmets were now strewn across the bridge, and fifty soldiers left dazed and confused.

I doubled back for the others who had conveniently kept their line nice and straight, and clobbered each of them on the back of the head, each one clanging as the suitcase made contact with metal.

Now the whole platoon was in total disarray, picking up helmets that didn't fit or belong to them, some staggering as if drunk and one fell over the side into the river.

I flew a victory roll over the confusion and screamed as loud as I could "Give that man a coconut!"

I couldn't resist it, Nasty was bawling at his men, his face so red I thought he might explode.

I glided down and hovered just above his head, then arched my neck down so my mouth was next to his ear!

"Hey Nasty!" He wheeled round, his great sword at the ready, but of course there was no one to be seen.

"Hey Nasty!" he turned even quicker this time, great veins were popping out on his sweaty forehead, he had turned a deep crimson colour.

Ranting and raving now, telling whoever it was to show themselves and fight like a man, not some cowardly demon.

Gently I landed just behind him and very carefully took the bottom of his skirt, pulled it up and tucked it into the top of his underpants, he was wearing pink undies!!

I knew that none of his men would dare tell him, and so that day they would be led into battle by a man exposing to all the world, his pink knickers.

I floated a few inches above his head to say my goodbyes "Bye, bye fish breath!" and soared off above the forest.

I could still see this little red faced figure screaming obscenities and waving his sword as I spotted the great hut, and descended to land safely just outside the door. "Hello Duncan, are you there?"

Something was wrong, he was supposed to be here, he was supposed to be ready .... something screaming leapt from behind me.

"Yaaaaarghhh!"

If you could compare a sight to a smell, then this was a visual version of Nasty's breath, it was like something from halloween night multiplied by fifty.

"Got you Master Raymond." said Duncan's voice from behind the green terror, "Well what do you think, will it scare them?"

"Duncan you nearly gave me a heart attack!"

"I am sorry Raymond, I just had to know if it worked before we face Nasticus," Still panting from the shock, I assured him

"Don't worry," it works, it definitely works, you've done a fantastic job Dunc, you really have."

"Now let's get you over by the large bowl and finish the job, the Romans are on their way!"

Within minutes Duncan and I were in position, a large leather belt belonging to Ram was fastened around my waist and Duncan's chest, securing me to him in a piggy back position.

I had hold of the hook to the coat hanger, which on this occasion was placed under the collar of Duncan's tunic. And there we were hovering above the tree tops, a boy from the 20th Century and a Druid from AD44, both completely invisible apart from the Druid's head.

And the Druids head, what a head it was!

In the time I was delaying the Romans, Duncan had painted his face green and dyed his hair and beard to match, he'd used darker shades under his eyes and in the hollows of his cheeks, which made him look gaunt and scary.

Using a twig as a brush he'd picked out the fine detail of the lines in his face in black, and topped it all of with a crown of leaves, the over all effect was incredible!

It was just how I imagined the Green Man to look, although nowhere near quite as frightening. If you were walking through the woods that day and happened to look up, all you would see is a magnificent green head, with long flowing green hair and beard, floating above the trees.

"Do you think everyone is ready and in position?"

"Oh I'm quite sure they will be Master Raymond, are you quite sure we won't fall out of the sky?"

"As sure as I can be," "Good, good, I'd be most grateful if we didn't," he was always so polite and that worried me.

"Listen Dunc, you're going to have to be really mean and horrible to Nasty and his soldiers, are you sure you're up to it?"

He gave a little laugh,

"Do you remember I told you it took twenty years to be trained as a fully fledged Druid?"

I nodded, realised he couldn't see me and said "Yes"

"And do you remember I told you I was best in my year at bursting boils and frostbite?"

"Yes" I replied once more,

"Well what I didn't tell you is that I was also best in my year at being a crazy, scary Druid, a talent often required in this job, although I've never actually used it yet."

I gulped "Here's your chance Dunc, look down there, the Romans are coming!"

21. The Battle for the Great Woods

Nasticus raised his right fist, "Company, halt!" and the now raggedy bunch of men clattered to a stop.

One or two of them were nervously pointing to Nasty's exposed rear end and giggling like school girls, the rest were peering anxiously deep into the woods, then on cue it began.

From somewhere in the distance or perhaps nearby, in fact the sound seemed to come from all around, an eerie wailing. "Wooooooooaaaarrrgghhh!" "Woooooooaaaarrrgghhh!"

Buried beneath piles of dead leaves were the children of the village's, all of them wailing just as we had rehearsed that morning in the hut. But now together, muffled by the leaves, echoing through the trees it was a sound to make your blood run cold.

Boom.....boom......boom a deep, slow heavy drum beat, rumbled through the woods adding to the complete spookiness of the scene, and then a metallic rattling sound. Strange! we hadn't planned any metallic rattling sounds.

It was the soldiers, the atmosphere of fear had really got to them, they were shaking in their sandals, breastplates, helmets and swords adding to the overwhelming din! This was going even better than I ever thought it would, now it was our turn.

I gently eased the coat hanger down and we slowly descended to where the soldiers were shaking, we could now hear Nasticus bawling at them to act like grown men not little babies.

"HA, HA, HA, HA, HA, HA, HAAARGHH!!" "HA, HA, HA, HA, HA, HA, HAAARGHH!!" Duncan laughed as we drew closer to them, it was the scariest laugh I had ever heard, it made me shiver, heaven knows how the soldiers below felt!

In between laughs he whispered to me "Told you, best in my year!" "You've got an audience Dunc, go get 'em!"

The whole of the Roman army were now staring skyward, transfixed by the awesome sight, I pulled back slightly and we hovered about ten feet off the ground and about the same distance away from where they stood.

He began in his best of year, scary Druid voice "Men of Rome, hear me and ignore me at your peril,"

I'd have given him an A+ just for that!

"I am the Green Man, protector of this wood and spirit guide to the Celts, my people have tolerated your ways far too long, so I must intercede on their behalf!"

"You are not welcome here, go in peace now," his voice deepened menacingly "Or face my wrath!"

Everyone of them was silent, unable to take in what was happening "What say you, Centurion?" bellowed the Druid,

causing them all including Nasty to visibly jump.

Nasticus somehow composed himself, stuck his chin out and stepped one pace forward, he was either extremely stupid or had loads of bottle and to his credit I think it was the latter.

"Listen spinach head, we're just gonna chop a few trees down, so why don't you just float off somewhere and get yerself a hair cut."

He was definitely brave and he was trying to build the confidence of his shaken men,

"These Britons hey lads, even their gods are scruffy," he laughed.

The soldiers never joined in the laughter, judging by their faces they were ready to take off and leave him, one or two of them looked quite worried that he was giving the Green Man so much lip!

The big soldier who'd got in a fight over his sandwich, was pushed forward by the rest, very gently he tapped Nasty on his shoulder.

"Excuse me sir, permission to speak.......it's just that me and the lads have had a bit of a chat and we think we should well, you know, do as Mr. Green Man says, if you know what I mean sir, thank you sir."

Nasty turned on him, veins popping out all over his forehead, small pieces of spit spraying everywhere as he screamed

"Get back in line you 'orrible little girly, the Roman army runs from nobody, and this bloke here has no body, just a scruffy green spinachy head."

"Now get your axes out and start chopping or so help me, I'll make you eat Celtic food for the rest of your stay in this miserable little excuse for a country!"

He turned back and faced us, with a smug smile,

"Still here, haven't you got the message yet you thick green lump of moss!"

That was it, I was mad now, proper mad, I pulled the coat hanger hard and we soared off in the direction of our starting position, high in the trees.

"Raymond, what on earth are we doing, this is not part of the plan!" I was too angry to give an explanation and as we banked at the end of the Great Wood shouted "Plans have changed!"

Nasty was laughing now "Look lads, old spinach head has done a runner, he's gone home to water his daisies!"

They still weren't laughing, because they could see that the green head had turned and was now heading at some considerable speed directly towards their leader with the pink undies.

They gazed open mouthed, speechless as the head zoomed closer and closer, eventually Nasty got the message and turned around just in time, to see Duncan's smiling face flying towards him.

For some reason Duncan said "Hello," and a fraction of a second later I made Nasticus eat suitcase! His legs flew high in the air and he crashed to the frozen earth with a sickening thud.

"Good shot master Raymond,"

we slowed, turned and returned to the spot where a very dazed centurion was trying to get back on his feet.

Duncan spoke, in one of his scariest voices

"I will not warn you again, leave this place and never return, NOW!!"

Nasticus stared at us defiantly and without turning to his troops, said quite calmly "If any man moves, he'll have to go through me."

The soldiers had nowhere to run, Nasty on one side the Green Man on the other, they huddled together in a shaking mass.

I placed my index finger and thumb between my lips and let out a high pitched whistle, it was time for phase two.

The soldiers couldn't see them and neither could we, but high in the trees to their left were Celtic warriors, Celtic warriors who'd recently had their first ever experience of soap.

Terrifying battle cries let loose and we knew that, at that very moment, they were swinging through the air on invisible ropes!

Suddenly the roman soldiers were tossed into the air and bowled over like skittles, by an invisible ball. Those still standing were in a state of shock, as they saw their fellow legionairres inexplicably flattened to the ground.

It was Ram's job to mop up these bemused troops, and one by one they fell too, eventually every soldier was lying confused and prostrate. Every soldier that is except Nasticus, I was saving the best until last.

The drum beats and wailing had ceased, now all that could be heard were the titters and giggling of small children.

This only served to make Nasticus even angrier, he strode through his men slapping, kicking and frightening them back onto their feet.

"Right you lot," he screamed red faced
"I want that great green bogey on the end of a spear, and I want it now, move yourselves!!!!"

They never moved, they just looked at him like he'd lost his marbles, he possibly had! He tried a different tack,

"Right, I see how it is, fine, all right six weeks leave on the island of Crete for the man who spears the scruffy spinach!" Now they were interested, every man held his spear in the air and they slowly but surely approached us.

Even if we flew off now, there was a very good chance that at least one of the hundred spears now aimed at us would be on target, a bead of sweat rolled down the side of my head.

Duncan gave a polite cough,
"I think now would be a good time master Raymond,"
"Now, what?" I whispered back,
"To whistle, to whistle!" he said with some urgency in his voice.

Of course, phase three, I was so scared I'd completely forgot, I put my fingers once more to my lips and blew, to my horror no sound came, I tried again, nothing. For some reason probably fear, my whistle had deserted me,
"I can't do it Dunc,"

"You must, you must, I can't whistle, it's not a Druid thing!"

There was only one thing for it, I cupped my hands around my mouth, took a deep breath and gave our gang call "Ooooooooooargh!" I just hoped the villagers would understand.

From deep in the woods I heard a 'Thwack,' 'Thwack'! and knew that they had. Earlier that morning while the children practiced their wailing, the Mum's were cooking a record breaking batch of porridge, which was now, courtesy of two branches, of two trees being pulled back acting as a catapult, flying through the air in the direction of our spear wielding aggressors.

One batch flew from the left and another from the right, both landing within seconds of each other, bang on target. The whole company of soldiers were completely covered in thick, grey, slimy porridge, it was all they could do to lift their sticky feet from the floor never mind throw spears.

"Can I get rid of this now, my arms are beginning to ache dreadfully," asked the Druid, "Yes, Dunc I think now would be a good time," and I directed the coat hanger to fly directly above Nasty's head.

One of the villager's owned a very old cow called Clover, and poor Clover had the 'trots' constantly,

Duncan had bravely collected a huge bucket full of this lovely smelly liquid and we were now ready to use it.

Standing slightly apart from his men Nasticus was as yet unblemished, "Centurion!" yelled Duncan and dutifully mouth wide open in shock Nasticus looked up.

The bucket of course had been washed in the soap, but the contents were quite visible and I truly hoped he never had time to close his mouth as the brown, green liquid pooh hit him square in the face!

Nasticus was completely coated in cow plop, I was sure I saw his bottom lip come out and heard him say the word Mummy as he ran screaming from the woods, quickly followed by his grey sticky men.

We watched them run, over the bridge, right past the fort, we watched as they got smaller and smaller, we watched until we could see them no more.

They wouldn't be coming back to this part of Briton, no Romans would.

22. Surprise! Surprise!

It was the first victory against the Roman army in living memory, Ram was delighted, laughing he threw me into the air, fortunately I had become visible again and he caught me safely in his huge hands.

"Ray Man you are a hero amongst my people, you must come and take wine with us tonight."

"I'm too young to drink, Mum would kill me!"

"Old enough to fight Romans, old enough to drink." And with that he slapped me on the back so hard I had to take two steps forwards.

He put his arm around me and walked me down to the river, "Look" he pointed downstream,

"One and a half Roman fort's but no soldiers, and it is because of you Ray Man, tonight there will be a great party in your honour."

"And what about the Druid?" I asked,

"Of course the mighty Druid was a great hero too, it will be a Ray Man and Druid party." I was worried and he could see it, so I asked

"Will there be porridge?"

he slapped me even harder on the back and I nearly ended up in the river again, Ram was doubled over in laughter

"You're a funny little hero Ray Man," with that I couldn't disagree.

It was about a half hour walk through the woods to the secret village, Duncan picked his way expertly through the trees with only the light of a wooden torch,

"Nearly there Raymond"

he said several times and I was beginning to think he was lost. And then suddenly the trees ended and we were facing a huge circular clearing, probably as large as four football pitches.

Lined up at the start of the clearing was every single person from both villages, warriors, women, old folk, children all standing in two long rows. As we were beckoned to walk down the middle they began to clap and cheer, warriors slapped us hard on the back, the Mum's and old ladies kissed our cheeks, the children just touched us and then ran back into the crowd.

We eventually emerged from the tunnel of praise, red faced but smiling, I had never helped so many people before, never made so many happy faces, it was a nice feeling. Perhaps this was the work that was so important to Freddy, I was glad now that I had risked all to get the suitcase, because it had created all this happiness.

The village was a magical sight, there were huge black metal poles all around complete with black metal bowls on top, each containing a small but roaring fire, a kind of AD44 version of street lighting.

Stone and thatch huts surrounded the circular clearing, each hut had coloured lanterns strung to the next hut, all the way around, and the centre piece was a huge bonfire crackling into the night sky.

Great long wooden tables were set out covered with all manner of food and drink, "Courtesy of our Roman friends." laughed Ram heartily,

"You could call it a leaving present." and we all joined in.

Ram made sure I had a goblet of wine, "To the Green Man." every one stood for the toast, they drained their goblets in one gulp and slammed them on the table.

"To Duncan." slam! "To Ray Man." slam! "To the Great Wood." slam! "To Porridge." slam! "To invisible soap." slam! "To Clover." slam! they toasted everyone and everything, they were rapidly becoming happier by the goblet!

Later there was singing and music, Duncan had toasted too many things and did his little Druid's jig, the children laughed at him, he didn't mind he was back with his people. Tomorrow they would build him a new hut in the village, they had faith in him once more and best of all he was no longer jobless.

It made me think of Dad and home, Mum would be worried silly, I missed my little sister, I missed my friends, I couldn't believe it but I even missed Mrs. Trickett and school.

I'd been gone for nearly three whole days, the police would be looking for me, my video's were overdue, Lenny would be in trouble.

I could see him in a dark cell, two burly policemen peppering him with questions.

"So Mr. Grimes, you say the victim jumped into an old brown suitcase and simply disappeared, surely you can come up with something better than that sonny!"

"Yes officer, I could but that's the truth."

"We've interviewed a number of your school friends, they say your famous for you're tall stories, is that correct sir?"

"No, I mean yes, but they were only stories, you know for a laugh."

"And I suppose you think it's funny to tell people there are bogeys in peanut butter?"

"Yes I suppose I do, but I never expected anyone to believe me."

"Then why should we believe you now Mr. Grimes?"

"Because it's the truth, he was there one minute and then he was gone, you've got to believe me!"

"I'm afraid nothing you have said would stand up in a court of law, so we have no alternative but to hold you, on suspicion of telling porkies!"

Poor Lenny looked gutted, I could see my Mum now, being consoled by a kindly policewoman.

"He's only wearing his pyjamas you know, the one's I bought him specially for having his tonsils out!" and she began to cry.

"You look far away master Raymond." I continued staring into the glowing embers of the bonfire.

"I was Dunc, I was back home, I think they'll be worried about me."
"Time is such a strange thing Raymond, it's a worm hole you know, your suitcase, it contains a worm hole and that is how you can travel through time."

"What on earth is a worm hole Duncan?" "I know not, but I do know it is a very precious thing, without it you would not be here now, this village would have been burnt to the ground, all these wonderful trees gone!"

"But more than any of this, I would not have had the great pleasure and honour of meeting Raymond Thursday and becoming his friend."

Only the heat from the fire stopped my eyes leaking down my cheeks, he went on,

"I saw it all in my dream, the man called Challenger took the worm hole from a terrible creature, who's only motive was to cause chaos and evil."

"The power of the suitcase must be held by someone honest and true, someone who's only wish is to help others, someone like you Raymond, I am sorry I'm becoming quite depressing, too many toasts I think!"

"The good news is, I'm fairly certain that when you return to your own time, it will in fact be the exact same instant you left."

"Really" I cheered up, "Really" he smiled back.
"But what about you oh mighty Druid, will the people keep their faith, will you keep your job?"

"I do believe I will, for I have given them a mighty gift!" "What is it?" "I have given the people football!" I smiled.

The Druid stood and offered me his hand "Come" he beckoned, "Where to," I asked

"Just come"

He grabbed my hand and gently pulled me upright, then led me into the woods, chattering excitedly, I didn't catch everything he said. "We've used the stone from the un-built fort, working from my notebook of course, it's nearly finished."

Reaching out he parted some branches, there was a clearing and a huge circular stone something! Duncan stood there hands on hips,

"Magnificent isn't it."

"What is it?" I enquired

"Raymond my boy, you are now looking at Briton's first and as yet only, all seater football stadium!"

"No" I gawped, "Yes it is, the warriors call it The Ray Man Stadium in honour of you."

"It's fantastic Dunc, the goals are a bit narrow though and a little high, usually they're made of wood not great massive lumps of stone."

"There are reasons, firstly the warriors want it to stand for generations as a tribute to our great victory and secondly nobody wants to play in goals, so we made them tall and narrow."

"That's fair enough, nobody wants to go in goals in my time either!" I was feeling exhausted and drained, "Would you mind if I went home now Duncan?"

Sadness swept over his face, he gulped "Of course not my boy, I am back with my people and you should be with yours."

I asked him to say goodbye to everyone for me, and told him I would like to come back and play football in my very own stadium one day soon,

"That would be grand, Raymond, just grand!" We were outside the wooden door of Duncan's hut,

"I'd like to give you a little present Dunc, something to remember me by," and I handed him a small piece of soap, "You never know when you might need it, especially if you are going to be the referee."

He thanked me and said he had a gift for me also and placed a small piece of folded paper in my hand,

"It's my very own porridge recipe, I know how much you like it!" we both laughed until it hurt.

"Come along lets get your case and get it over with, I really do hate goodbyes" he pushed through the door and lit the lantern inside, warm light slowly flickered into life and that was the last thing Duncan saw for some time.

"I knew it was you two." a familiar voice came from the shadows and with frightening speed a fist hit Duncan full in the face, he flew over the table and lay on the floor motionless. Heart beating madly I ran to his fallen body and cradled his head in my arms, he was breathing but he was out cold.

"One down, one to go!" That voice, I recognised it, I looked up to see the face that belonged to the voice emerge from the shadows, the face of Nasticus!

23. Time to go Home

I was scared out of my wits, but at the same time very angry and blurted out

"If you've hurt him, I'll!".............

"You'll do nothing boy," he yelled his eyeballs practically bursting from their sockets and looking like a crazed animal. He slowly circled us, sword in hand, in the other he was casually tossing and catching a ball, that terrible smug smile a permanent feature on his still stained face.

"I think by now all your Celtic friends will be sleeping off the wine they stole from the fort, so you see you're all alone, there's no one to help you."

"Y'know I sensed you were trouble the moment I found you shivering on that hillside, should have run you through with my blade there and then, could have saved myself all this trouble."

"We knocked the fight out of these Celts years ago and once they'd banished the old Druid, we knew they were a broken people."

"Make's them much easier to manage, the last thing they needed was hope, that just causes problems."

"Who could have given them hope?"

"It had to be someone from the outside, it had to be you, so tell me who are you boy and where are you from?"

"I'm a Briton," I said defiantly!

"I think not, your ways are foreign and you speak with a strange tongue, that is how you gave yourself away."

"This morning when you taunted me at the bridge, I see you do not remember your words, let me remind you."

He lowered his face a few inches from mine and screamed at me "Bye bye fish breath!"

I thought I would throw up, his breath was worse than ever and I knew in that moment without a shadow of doubt that he hadn't managed to close his mouth in time, when we covered him in Clover pooh.

Duncan stirred slightly and made a groaning sound.

"Aha the Druid is coming around, good, good, you can watch him die first," he continued to circle us, "Can you catch boy!" Without warning he threw the ball at me hard, and I saw his disappointment as I caught it easily, holding it up with my free hand I saw it wasn't a ball, it was an onion!

His terrible smile grew larger,

"Do you know something, in all the excitement today I do believe I missed dinner, now what goes well with onion, hmmmmm I have it, LIVER!"

Oh my giddy aunts, I couldn't believe it, he really was going to eat my liver! I went dizzy and weak, if I'd been standing I'm sure I would have fallen. Suddenly he strode towards us raising his sword in both hands, no longer smiling his face was a picture of pure hatred.

"Now you die and then I burn these cursed woods to the ground and everything in them, say goodbye to the Druid!"

The Druid wasn't for saying goodbye just yet, he hadn't let on, but had regained consciousness and as Nasticus was about to bring down the mighty weapon upon Duncan's stricken body, he stuck out a leg and swept the Roman's feet from beneath him.

The Druid jumped to his feet with great speed, pushing me behind him as he did so, at the same time Nasticus was slowly rising from the floor, his evil eyes fixed menacingly on my friend.

"That was your last mistake old man." growled Nasticus,

Duncan half turned his head towards me,

"Get the suitcase and go Raymond."

"But Duncan, I can't leave you like this."

Duncan edged us back towards the door and the suitcase, using his body as a shield between Nasticus and myself.

"Raymond go!"

"I won't, I won't, not like this!"

Nasticus made the most of his opportunity, he'd picked up a wooden stool and threw it in our direction, Duncan turned too late and it caught him hard on the side of the head.

He wobbled slightly, fell to his knees, managed one word "Go!" then collapsed in a heap on the floor.

I raised my head to see Nasticus picking up his sword and smiling at me, that evil smile. I pulled back my right arm and threw with every last bit of strength in my body, my aim was true, the onion hit Nasty square on the nose.

He yelped like a wounded animal and grabbing my suitcase I was out of the door, running, running my breath visible in the cold night air.

I could hear the sound of bracken and branches being broken under foot, close behind me. I couldn't run any faster, I was exhausted from the last few days, it would only be a matter of time before he caught me.

I had an idea, still running I swung my case several time above my head and launched it into the night sky in front of me. As it sailed silently through the air, I mustered up my last remaining breath and shouted,

"Yad Sruht Dnom Yar!"

It slowly began to open leaving a trail of sparkly gold in its path, I just needed it to land the right way up, or I was finished.

It landed, bounced, turned over several times and came to rest at the base of a tree, it was the right way up!

Nasticus was screaming close behind me, I knew he must be really close as I could now smell him, I set myself, took two large steps and dived headlong into the open suitcase.

Whoooosh! Total darkness and total silence, I was in what Duncan called the worm hole. Whoooosh! I flew headfirst out of the case, tripped over and fell flat on my face on my bedroom carpet, as it turned out it was fortunate that I did.

Duncan had been right, Lenny was still stood there, cardboard tube in hand still laughing his head off, seeing me lying on the floor, muddy and no longer wearing my pyjamas, he stopped bemused and speechless.

From somewhere in the distance came a screaming sound, gradually becoming louder and louder, I realised too late what it was.

Whoooosh! He was here, he must have dived after me into the

suitcase, Nasticus was in my bedroom! He'd landed right in front of the telly, a strange sight for someone from AD44, the 'Beast from Mars' was crunching more soldiers and roaring angrily at the tanks and jet planes.

Very slowly I stretched my hand out, Nasticus was transfixed by the sight in front of him, got it! I pumped the volume up to maximum on the remote control and the scaly monster provided his best roar of the whole film.

Nasty took a couple of steps backwards, tripped and fell pink undies first into the suitcase and disappeared.

I dived across the room slammed the lid down and buckled the fasteners to the suitcase, 'When jumping, close the door behind you,' the list really was complete now.

Breathing the biggest sigh of relief in the history of the world, I walked towards Lenny, placed two fingers under his chin and gently closed his gaping mouth. It was a while before Lenny could think straight, let alone talk, but once he started he hardly drew breath.

We turned the telly off, and over the next few hours I told him everything.

"I believe you Ray, I really do, it's too weird for you or anyone to make up."

I made him promise not to tell anyone, but even if he did no one would believe Lenny.

"I'm absolutely shattered Len, would you go down and get our drinks from the fridge?"

"Sure, Ray," he got half way across the room when he let out a loud "Ouch!" and then proceeded to dance about on one leg.

"Ray, I think your friend left something!"

I jumped down from the top bunk to see Nasty's jewel handled sword lying on my bedroom floor.

"Oh no, how am I going to explain that to Mum and Dad, it's bad enough I left my pyjamas and slippers back in AD44!"

Lenny asked if he could keep it, I told him he couldn't as people would ask questions, the only thing to do was bury it in the garden.

And so in the early hours of the morning, under the light of a friendly 20th Century moon, we disposed of the evidence. It was good to be back.

If you could jump into my suitcase and pop out again in this same room but six months into the future, you would find a lot of changes. If I were here in my old bedroom I would tell you this. That I forgot Dad was obsessed with digging the garden and guess what, he found the sword!

Turned out to be the best example of a Centurions sword ever found and was sold at auction for £177,000. Which means I suppose that we are quite well off, we've moved to a bigger house not far from our old one, so I still see Lenny and all my friends.

Dad got a new car, Mum's having the Moggie, I got my new bike and Jo can now count to three.

Strange how things turn out, Nasticus was intent on eating my liver, but instead he changed all our lives for the better.

Dad no longer stares, in fact he's started his own business as a landscape gardener and is busy all the time. We still have our day trips out at weekends, he's just like the Dad he used to be, if not better.

Oh yes, I almost forgot he's bought himself a metal detector and we go looking for treasure, we've got a great collection of ring pulls.

I took Lenny flying with the coat hanger last week, I don't think he really believed me until we took off, he loved it. I came top of the class in History, a subject I never excelled at, but it has come alive now and I want to know more and more.

I think often of Duncan, Ram and the villagers, I also think of Nasticus and wonder where the suitcase sent him. My favourite imaginings are of him being chased by dinosaurs in the Jurassic period, that one always makes me laugh.

I hope you enjoyed my story, it wasn't told purely for entertainment but more as a record, a record of the suitcase and it's power and a record of Raymond Thursday.

Why should there be a record of Raymond Thursday you ask? I shall tell you, tonight when Mum and Dad are fast asleep, I have decided it is time to jump back into the suitcase. I have no idea where it will take me or if I will return, but at least you will know why I have disappeared from the face of this planet.

You would of course have to practice saying your own name backwards, before you too could become a time traveller.

So while you practice I'll get back to the night Lenny and I had buried the sword and crept quietly back to my bedroom.

We both lay in our bunks, too tired to sleep,
"Lenny,"
"Yeah,"
"You asleep yet,"
"No,"
"I forgot to tell you something,"
"Oh yeah."
"Well you know Stonehenge,"
"Yeah,"
"You know nobody really knows what it is,"
"Yeah"
"I do"
"Oh yeah, what?"
"It's Britain's first ever all-seater football stadium!"
"Shuddup Ray, and go to sleep!"